Dear Reader,

I don't know anybody who hasn't dreamed this at one time or another. To be marooned on a tropical island with the man of your dreams— heaven!

Add to that fact that I'm a big fan of survival and wildlife shows, especially the ones where the presenters are so cheerful and unruffled as they ramble on about poisonous plants or marauding herds, while pointing out the volcano behind them that's due to erupt at any moment or the piranha-infested river they're planning to kayak, just as soon as they've splinted the leg of this cute little snarling puma.

Writing this book was a dream because I got to create my own heart-melting presenter and also to wonder how I might fare in a survival situation—though I freely admit I didn't take my research as far as eating bugs!

So sit back and enjoy this feast of sand, sea and s... Well, I'll say no more. Slap on that sunscreen and enjoy the adventures of the indomitable Jessie Banks!

Best wishes,

Samantha Connolly

She was just tired, that was it. That had to be it.

Jessie's eyes widened as Nick unbuttoned his shirt. Had she been completely wrong about him? About this show? Was she expected to have sex with him after all? On camera?

"Here," said Nick, handing her his shirt. "Put this on. It'll give your things time to dry."

Jessie was mortified by her assumptions and touched by his consideration. She took the shirt and slipped it on.

"I just wanted to tell you that you don't have to worry about bunking together tonight.... I mean, uh, that's not something you, uh..."

So much for her ego. Jessie said awkwardly, "Uh, oh, you neither, of course."

"Let's get some sleep. Big day tomorrow."

Nick seemed devoid of any awkwardness as he lay down on the cot and curved his arm around her. She snuggled against him and could feel the steady rise and fall of his chest. Meanwhile, her heart was thudding like a piston.

Suddenly Jessie decided that she didn't care if the others *were* less than ten feet away. She was in bed with Nick Garrett—gorgeous, kind, hugely popular TV host—and she was going to make the most of it.

i will
survive

Samantha
Connolly

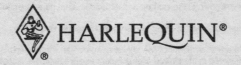

HARLEQUIN®

TORONTO • NEW YORK • LONDON
AMSTERDAM • PARIS • SYDNEY • HAMBURG
STOCKHOLM • ATHENS • TOKYO • MILAN • MADRID
PRAGUE • WARSAW • BUDAPEST • AUCKLAND

ISBN 0-373-44182-7

I WILL SURVIVE

Copyright © 2004 by Samantha Connolly.

This edition published by arrangement with Harlequin Books S.A.

® and TM are trademarks of the publisher. Trademarks indicated with ® are registered in the United States Patent and Trademark Office, the Canadian Trade Marks Office and in other countries.

Visit us at www.eHarlequin.com

Printed in U.S.A.

ABOUT THE AUTHOR

Born in Ireland, Samantha Connolly has lived all over the globe. Her family (mom, dad, younger sister) moved to Australia when she was four. Six years later the family returned to their native Ireland, where her parents opened their own bookshop. And there Samantha's love affair with books began. Growing up surrounded by books, she dreamed of writing one of her own someday. After completing university, she lived in London for several years, working in a number of places, including an art gallery. And she earned her private pilot's license (now sadly expired due to lack of flying hours, but she plans on retaking the exams one day!). Samantha, too, has now returned to Ireland and gotten serious about her writing. She divides her time between putting pen to paper and working in her family's bookstore. Her hobbies include horseback riding, camping and, of course, reading.

Books by Samantha Connolly

HARLEQUIN DUETS
86—IF THE SHOE FITS
104—A REAL WORK OF ART

This one's for Kathryn Lye
Editor extraordinaire
Whose persistently high standards
both exasperate me beyond measure
and make me write better than I knew I could

For all the many times you've made me
want to throw my laptop out the window
My deepest thanks

1

JESSIE BANKS STEPPED out of the tiny bathroom and looked crossly at the other occupant of the small cabin.

"This is ridiculous," she said. "I won't wear this."

Lois ran her eyes appraisingly over Jessie. "But you look fantastic. It's perfect on you." She moved out of the way to allow Jessie to look at herself in the full-length mirror. Jessie spread her arms.

"Oh, you're right," she said. "What was I thinking? This is indeed the perfect outfit for ten days on a desert island."

The yacht crested a wave and Jessie teetered on her five-inch heels.

"That's the spirit," said Lois, deliberately ignoring Jessie's sarcasm.

Jessie sighed and pointed at the cargo pants and checked shirt that were strewn across the bunk bed.

"Is the joke over now?" she said. "Can I put my own clothes back on?"

Lois raised one perfectly plucked eyebrow and her gaze turned steely. "Look, a shipwreck is an unexpected thing, right? When it happens you don't really have the luxury of picking and choosing what you're going to wear."

"I'm aware of that," retorted Jessie. "But even if I can't wear my own clothes is it really necessary for me to be dressed like a...well, a lady of the night?"

"Don't be ridiculous," scoffed Lois. "That's a designer dress."

Jessie pulled up one of the spaghetti straps that had slipped off her shoulder. "It may well be a designer dress," she said in despair, "but it still feels like it'll fall apart before we even get to the island. I don't see how it'll last the whole ten days."

"So that can be one of your projects on the island, to fashion yourself some new clothes."

"Let me guess," said Jessie. "Coconut shells and a grass skirt?"

"Whatever you like," said Lois impassively.

Jessie turned back to the mirror again and gazed at her implausible attire. The red dress, which stopped a good four inches above her knees, was made of some kind of stretchy, spangled material that hugged every curve of her figure. It was a figure that was usually hidden by her demure tailored suits at work or played down in jeans and loose-fitting chambray shirts at home but even in those innocuous clothes it could still only be described as statuesque. And with the strappy shoes bringing her height to almost six feet she was barely able to stand up in the cramped cabin.

She turned back to Lois, polite but determined.

"I'm sorry but this is not going to work. I'm not wearing it and you can't make me."

Lois riffled through the sheaf of papers she was holding and thrust a few pages towards Jessie.

"Actually, we can."

"What's this?"

"It's a complete copy of the rules, terms and conditions of the competition, which, in entering, you agreed to abide by."

Jessie flipped through the pages, squinting at the dense print. "I never saw these."

Lois shrugged. "Contestants were invited to send away for the full rules if they so wished. Have a look at Section Two, Part Four."

Jessie read aloud. "The attire and accoutrements of the participants, aka competition finalists, shall be determined at the sole and total discretion of Quest Broadcasting."

Jessie looked up and waved the rules at Lois. "I don't suppose there's any other little surprises in here that I should know about, is there? Any little clauses saying I have to sleep with Nick Garrett by any chance?"

Lois let out a fake laugh. "What you want to get up to on the island is entirely up to you." She shrugged. "Of course something like that wouldn't hurt the ratings."

Jessie gave her a narrow-eyed look which didn't appear to faze the producer in the slightest. "So," she said brightly to Jessie. "I'm afraid you do it our way or not at all."

Jessie looked back at the mirror, struggling with her decision.

She had long been an avid fan of *Survive This!*—the TV show where the charismatic presenter and survival expert, Nick Garrett, spent each week in a different situation. Whether it was wilderness or rainforest, desert or arctic, Nick showed the viewers how to find water, create fire, build shelters and subsist on the indigenous wildlife. And as if it wasn't enough that he had all that skill and expertise, the guy was also charming and funny and just an all-round, total hunk.

In contrast, Jessie's practical survival knowledge was nil. There wasn't much call for a small-town librarian to go trapping wild rabbits, building rafts or knowing the correct smoke signals to attract search-and-rescue teams. That didn't stop her from reading every book she could find on the subject or harboring a secret certainty that, should an emergency situation arise, she'd be able to acquit herself admirably.

When Nick had announced that they were putting together a special show whereby members of the public would be selected to enact a survival situation on a tropical island she'd realized immediately that she had no chance of being picked. But she'd amused herself by entering the competition anyway, sending off the requested essay, photograph, and biographical details. She'd nearly gone into cardiac arrest when Nick had reeled off her name on the program, along with the two other people that she would be competing against for the grand prize of a million dollars.

A flight to L.A., then into the offices of Quest Broadcasting and, after another flight to Tahiti, she had boarded the yacht that was currently speeding her towards an isolated, uninhabited island.

She couldn't back out, not after coming this far. To spend a fortnight with Nick Garrett on a tropical island, even without the incentive of the prize money, was an unmissable opportunity. Both for the sake of an unforgettable adventure and also to see if Nick really was as funny and captivating as he always seemed on the show.

Okay, the fact that there'd be a camera following them around was a little unnerving but, up to this moment, hadn't proved a sufficient deterrent.

Because, of course, she hadn't imagined herself appearing on the nation's television screens dressed quite like this.

She gave Lois one last beseeching look. "Are you sure you don't have anything else I could wear?"

"That's it," said Lois impassively. "Take it or leave it."

Jessie laughed weakly. "It's going to look pretty strange wearing my backpack over this."

"It sure is," agreed Lois. "Which is why you won't be. Attire *and* accoutrements," she reminded Jessie. She pointed to a small purse on the bed. "You can take that evening bag. It matches your dress."

"But..." Jessie faltered. "You mean I'll have no equipment? No supplies? Nothing?"

Lois folded her arms and gave a sigh to emphasize how

very patient she was being. "Look, I don't see how I can make this any clearer. You know the premise. You're on a cruise ship and it goes down in the middle of the ocean. You, Nick and the others are washed ashore on a desert island. Lucky for you Nick is a survival expert. You guys, however, are just civilians. I mean, let's face it, anyone could manage if they were washed up with a bag full of survival gear, couldn't they?"

Jessie felt herself wavering. She had to admit that Lois was making a good point. "I guess you're right," she said at last.

"Great," said Lois. "Well, let's get this show on the road. Or, should I say, into the water. You ready to go?"

"I just have to use the bathroom."

Lois nodded. "Okay, then come straight up on deck." She made for the door.

Jessie kept the smile on her face until Lois left the cabin but then she quickly replaced it with a look of determination.

She grabbed the sparkly purse and shuffled through the contents.

Perfume, lipstick, a compact and condoms.

Jessie rolled her eyes.

Keeping one ear cocked for the sounds of anyone approaching she rummaged in her backpack and pulled out some of the things that she'd prided herself on packing. Penknife, a mini compass, sunscreen; one by one she squashed them into the bag. A tiny sewing kit, she'd definitely be needing that. She opened the perfume bottle and, without so much as a blink, poured fifty dollars worth of scent down the sink. She rinsed the bottle and refilled it with something much more useful. She rolled up the lipstick and snapped it off at the base. Ten waterproof matches fit perfectly inside the tube. She put the perfume bottle, the compact and the lipstick into the bag and held the condoms for a moment, vacillating, before she eventually tucked them back in, too, reasoning that they didn't really take up any room.

JESSIE HAD TO SHADE her eyes as she climbed up the narrow stairwell to the deck of the yacht. The sun was dazzling and the sky and sea seemed to be competing to show off how blue they could be. Jessie gasped as she spotted, looming on the horizon, a breathtakingly beautiful island. Green forest flowed down to the golden beaches and birds wheeled overhead.

There were about twenty people on deck and Jessie stood awkwardly, holding onto the handrail, trying to ignore the sidelong glances and startled whispers that her appearance had provoked.

Lois beckoned her over to the side of the yacht. After a pause Jessie let go of the handrail and tottered over on the spiky heels. She fell forward to grab the side-rail as she reached Lois.

"Good grief," she complained. "These shoes are hazardous." She lowered her voice and spoke plaintively to Lois. "I feel like an idiot."

Lois waved her hand dismissively at the people milling around. "Oh, they're just crew and staff, forget about them. This is who I want you to meet. Jessie, say hello to Kenny, our on-site cameraman. Kenny will be following you and the others with the handheld."

Jessie smiled and looked with yearning at his baseball hat, sloppy jeans and checked shirt.

"Hey, that's a great dress, man," he said, greeting her with the kind of complex hand signal that she had only ever seen MTV presenters use.

"Er, yes," she said. "Thanks...Kenny."

Lois waved her hand towards the sea. "So, what do you think of your island?"

Jessie grinned unabashedly. "It's amazing. I can't believe this is happening. I don't know if what I'm feeling is excitement or terror. This is it, it's real."

"You bet it is," said Lois. She held out a pair of binoculars. "Here, take a look, the others are waiting for you."

Jessie took the binoculars and scanned the shoreline. She zeroed in on the three people standing on the beach and she breathed in as she recognized Nick Garrett.

It was really him! At the first glimpse of that unmistakable tanned face and dark blond hair Jessie felt her heart grab before it kick-started again with a thud. Nick's arms were folded and he was nodding as he listened to the man next to him, his dark brows dipping into a concentrated frown, shadowing his eyes. Jessie realized she was holding her breath and she let it out, wondering what she was going to say when she actually met him. Just say hello, she told herself, tell him how much you like the show but be normal. Please don't start giggling or fawning or anything embarrassing like that.

She lowered the binoculars as she realized that Lois was talking to her.

"It's a pity we had that trouble with your flight but don't worry about it. The others have already had one night on the island but we won't be officially starting the competition until tomorrow anyway. I'm sure you'll have plenty of time to get settled in. Now, what we're going to do is drop you into the water about a quarter mile from shore. Your bio said you could swim?"

Jessie nodded.

"Anyway, Kenny and I will be alongside in a motorboat so you won't be in any danger, we just want to get the shot of you, literally, washing up on shore."

Jessie nodded again, too nervous to speak.

THE WATER WAS WARM and the sun glinted sparkles into her eyes as she was lowered into the sea. She had looped the evening bag over her shoulder and across her chest and it bobbed alongside her.

She treaded water for a moment, feeling her muscles loosen and then struck out for shore. At least her dress and shoes didn't weigh her down, which was about the only good thing that could be said for them.

She heard the thrum of the motorboat and paused, treading water again as it came up beside her.

"How are you doing?" said Lois, yelling to be heard above the sound of the idling motor.

"Fine," called back Jessie.

"Okay, we're right here if you need help. You look great."

Jessie looked at Kenny whose face was hidden behind the camera and he gave her a thumbs-up. She grinned and turned back towards the island. She struck out resolutely, getting closer to the dream island with each pull of her long arms. Her mind was flitting about wildly. She wondered what the other contestants would be like and what sort of challenges they were all going to face. Would they be at each other's throats at the end of the ten days or would they have made friends for life? Was there any hope at all that she might even win the money?

She was about thirty meters from shore when she felt the strap of her evening bag slip off her shoulder and down over her arm. She grabbed wildly for it but it glided through her fingers and down around her waist. She could feel the bag knocking against her ankle and she knew she'd have to catch it before it had a chance to slip away entirely.

She stopped, kicking rhythmically to keep her head above water while her hands swept around her, clutching for either the bag or the strap. She glanced towards the shore and she saw Nick come down towards the shoreline. She waved reassuringly and dipped her hands under again to search for the bag.

She couldn't feel anything so she took a deep breath and ducked her head under the surface, searching for the glittering prize. The strap was caught on her shoe and she struggled with it, trying to unhook it. She came up, treading water while she caught her breath. The sun flashed off the water, dazzling her and she ducked under again, clutching at her foot. The strap had wound around her ankle so it was almost a minute before she got it off and she burst her head to the surface again, gasping for breath. She shook the water from her face, her heart thumping with triumph and she gulped in lungfuls of air to pump her up for the last stretch.

Suddenly she was yanked forcefully through the water as a huge arm was thrust around her neck.

"It's okay, I've got you," came Nick's voice in her ear. Spumes of water sprayed on either side of her face as he tugged her along in a lifesaving grip.

Jessie spluttered as she caught a mouthful of water and she tugged at his muscular forearm, trying to break free. She opened her mouth to tell him she was okay but another splash caught her, setting off a fit of coughing. Nick swam like a shark, dragging her body along as if she were nothing more than a rag doll and eventually she just gave up trying to escape because his grasp was unbreakable. He was obviously intent on saving her so she just clung grimly to his arm as his strong legs kicked between hers. She caught a glimpse of the boat speeding along beside them and she tried to signal to Lois and Kenny that she was all right but they didn't appear to notice and Nick just seemed to take her flailing arms as a sign of further distress because he tightened his grip and swam all the harder.

She was coughing again by the time they reached the shore and a sudden wave of dizziness overcame her as he laid her down on the sand. She closed her eyes against the glare of the sun and concentrated on getting her breath back. She became aware of Nick's hand on her throat, checking her pulse.

"She's okay," he called as the motorboat pulled up onto the sand.

Jessie gasped as he lay his head down across her chest. She could feel water from his hair dripping onto her bare skin. "Good breath sounds," he went on. "No water in there. I think she's just fainted."

"Excuse me," said Jessie archly, "I haven't fainted and would you mind getting your head off my chest."

Nick's head rose sharply and Jessie struggled to sit up. "I haven't fainted because I wasn't even in trouble in the first place. I was just..." She broke off, searching the sand around her. "Oh, no, my bag, where is it?"

"What?" said Nick in bemusement.

Jessie clambered to her feet, unceremoniously using Nick's shoulder as a prop. "My bag," she said insistently. "I don't believe this, you lost it."

"Are you okay?" he said.

She looked at him. "Am I okay?" she said derisively. "Of course I'm okay. For your information tough guy, I was doing just fine until you came along." She pointed out towards the ocean. "I was just treading water and trying to catch my bag when you came storming up and almost killed me. What on earth were you thinking?"

He stood up, eyes flashing. "What was I thinking? Oh, I don't know, maybe when I see someone struggling in the water I just assume that they could use some help. Why did you wave at me if you weren't in trouble?"

"I was just waving hello!" Jessie exclaimed, her embarrassment making her defensive.

"You've got to be kidding me," he said angrily. "You stop

swimming to wave hello and then you sink underwater a couple of times just for good measure? What is that, your idea of a joke?"

She was about to fire back another retort when she spotted a familiar red shape that was rolling in the small waves nearby.

"My bag," she cried gleefully, stumbling towards it.

"Oh, great," said Nick, following her. "You found your bag. I'm so glad. We wouldn't want you to go through the next ten days without your makeup."

She made a face at him and bent over to pick up the bag. Unfortunately she caught it by the bottom and released the contents in a shower as she lifted it. She fell to her knees and grabbed at the sewing kit as it tried to float away on a wave and she dug the penknife out of the wet sand before thrusting them back into her purse.

Nick's voice came from above her. "Don't forget these."

She turned her head and her gaze traveled up his long legs to see the condoms that he was holding out to her.

She snatched them out of his hand, not even looking at him and shoved them crossly into the bag.

Nick turned on his heel and stomped away from her. "Lois, you and I need to talk, right now," he said.

"Be right there, Nick," said Lois. She turned to Kenny, her eyes shining with excitement. "Did you get all that?"

Another thumbs-up from Kenny. Lois clenched her fists triumphantly. "This is great television," she exclaimed, trotting after Nick.

Jessie put her head in her hands. Welcome to paradise.

JESSIE UNDID THE STRAPS of her shoes and took them off before she stood up. Okay, that was a start. There were strands of hair sticking to her face and she wiped them back while she looked properly for the first time at the two people who were going to be her companions for the next ten days, as well as her competition.

"Hi, there," said the woman. "Is that your own dress?"

Jessie looked down. "Gosh, no. There's no way I would have worn this."

"It's beautiful," said the woman. "I wish they'd given it to me." She put out her hand. "I'm Cindi Todd. That's *Cindi* with an *i*."

Jessie shook hands with her, frowning slightly. "Isn't *Cindy* usually spelt with an *i*?"

The two women looked at each other.

"I mean, with an *i* at the end," said Cindi.

"Oh, okay." Jessie nodded. She laughed. "So it's really Cindi with two *i*s."

Cindi's smile tightened. "I've found that people usually know what I mean."

Jessie raised her eyebrows at the condescending tone and there was an awkward pause before Cindi spoke again, pointing down at her own attire. "I think I'm supposed to be one of the ship's crew. A chambermaid or cabin-maid or whatever they call it." She was wearing a fitted black uniform with a white apron. It had long sleeves, Jessie noticed jealously.

She doubted that "Cindi with an *i*" was a chambermaid in real life. She had the look of someone who spent a lot of money looking after herself. Her short, platinum, tousled hair emphasized her big eyes, full lips and Slavic cheekbones. She was five and a half feet of slender, toned perfection and she made Jessie feel gangly and clumsy.

It didn't help that Jessie was also an inch or two taller than the other contestant.

The man pushed his glasses up on his snub nose before he spoke.

"I'm Malcolm Talbot," he said. "From Denver, Colorado."

"Nice tuxedo," said Jessie. It probably had been nice originally, and on a handsome man it might have looked rakish and dissolute, but Malcolm didn't look as if he'd be comfortable in a tuxedo at the best of times. With his round face, receding hairline and owlish glasses he simply looked disheveled and lost.

"Did you guys get 'washed-up,' too?" asked Jessie.

Cindi and Malcolm looked at each other.

"Uh...no," Cindi said apologetically. "We were brought to the shore."

"I'm not a very good swimmer," added Malcolm. "So I probably couldn't have done it anyway."

Jessie could see that he was trying to make her feel better and she smiled in appreciation.

"It really was quite a long swim," chimed in Cindi. "You shouldn't be embarrassed about getting into trouble."

"But I didn't," said Jessie. She kept her voice pleasant but spoke firmly. "I only stopped because I thought I'd dropped my bag. I didn't actually need to be rescued." She turned to Kenny who was hovering silently nearby. "I mean, you were filming it. You saw that I wasn't drowning, right?" She paused, waiting for an answer. "Kenny?"

Kenny's head came away from the camera's eyepiece and he grimaced apologetically. "Uh...I'm not really supposed to talk, you know. I'm just like, an independent observer. Just pretend I'm not here."

"It's okay," Cindi said reassuringly. "I don't have a clue about any of this survival stuff, either." She shrugged. "That's what we have the men for, right?"

Jessie's mouth fell open but before she could respond, Malcolm spoke up.

"I've got lots of survival books at home and I love Nick's show. I mean, I've never done anything like this before but I really wanted to come. Then, last night, we had to build our own shelters and go and find water and purify it. It was great!"

His eyes lit up as he talked and Jessie got the first inkling that Malcolm might actually be fun to be around.

Cindi laughed at his enthusiasm and put her hand on his arm. "Perfect! You can feel free to help me out any time you want. I won't argue."

"I'm really looking forward to doing stuff like that, too," insisted Jessie, trying not to sound belligerent. "I think that's part of the fun of being here."

"Oh, I see," said Cindi thoughtfully. "You guys are here for fun." She lifted her eyebrows into two wicked darts. "It's got nothing to do with winning a million bucks?"

Both Jessie and Malcolm laughed out loud.

"Let's face it," said Cindi, "we'll probably end up back-stabbing and betraying each other at the end but at least we can start out as friends, right?"

Jessie grinned, her misgivings about Cindi falling away. The girl was brash but at least she was up front about it.

"I'll be honest with you," Cindi went on, "I really don't care about the money."

"Yeah, right," scoffed Jessie cheerfully.

"No, really," laughed Cindi. "I'm in it for the fame. I've been trying to get my break as an actress for years and you can't beat this kind of exposure."

Malcolm and Jessie looked at each other.

"I believe her." Malcolm shrugged. "I'm not really in it for the money, either. I just want to prove to myself that I can do it."

Jessie spread her arms. "This is great. I *am* in it for the money, so why don't we just agree that I'm the winner?"

Malcolm laughed. "I would but my wife would kill me. She's pregnant and a million dollars would make a great nest egg."

"Ooh, congratulations," cooed Jessie and Cindi. Emboldened by their interest, Malcolm pulled out a photograph which was tucked into a small, plastic sleeve. "This is my Debbie," he said bashfully. "That's us on our honeymoon, in Miami."

"She's lovely," said Jessie. Okay, Debbie wouldn't be gracing the cover of *Vogue* anytime soon, but the couple had their arms around each other and the Malcolm in the photo looked just as besotted as the one standing in front of them. "You two look really happy."

"We are," said Malcolm, taking back the photo. "Married almost three years."

"No husband or kids for me, thank you," said Cindi. "I like the single life way too much. How about you, Jessie?" She picked up Jessie's hand. "I don't see a ring. You married? Or got anyone special?"

Jessie hesitated. That question would have been so much easier to answer only twenty-four hours earlier.

She was thinking about what to say when she realized that both Cindi and Malcolm were looking past her shoulders. She turned to see Nick bearing down on them, Lois hot on his heels.

2

JESSIE STRAIGHTENED HER spine and licked her lips nervously as Nick and Lois re-joined them. Kenny circled around so he could catch Nick's arrival.

"Okay," said Lois, crackling with authority. "Jess and Nick, I love this sexual tension thing you two have got going on and we'll really play on it later but, for now, let's just put it on hold until we get the practicalities sorted out."

Jessie was horrified, even more so when Cindi nudged her and made kissy noises.

"There's no sexual tension," Jessie and Nick said in unison and then their eyes met in dismay.

Lois laughed delightedly. "Right," she said. "Obviously. Anyway, I'm going to give you the rundown and I'm only saying it once so listen up everyone. We're trying to keep the camera presence as unintrusive as possible. Even though this is a special we're maintaining the feel of the regular *Survive This!* show, so Kenny will be the only handheld following you. Unless you have to split up and then we'll bring in temps. Apart from that there are cameras scattered around the island." She smiled. "We call them the Island Eyes."

"Where are they?" asked Jessie.

"You don't need to know. Now, you've also got the confession cam in the tiki hut, which is beyond the coconut trees at the end of the beach. Contractually, you're obligated to do ten minutes, twice a day, but you can go in more often if you like. Remember, it's no-holds-barred in there. Talk about life on the island, each other, what's happening, any problems you're having. If you're thinking it, we want to hear about it." She waggled her finger at them. "No holding out on us. And remember, that's also your chance to address the audience directly. Which leads me nicely on to my next point."

She looked down, checking her clipboard. "Nick will be setting challenges for you while you're here and there'll be a certain amount of points going for those. But sixty percent of your scores will come from audience votes so in the end, they're the ones who will really be deciding who wins."

Jessie nodded along with the others and then risked a peek at Nick. He was looking down at the sand, apparently listening, and she let her gaze linger on his face. The blue-green eyes framed with dark lashes, the thick tousled hair, the laugh lines at the corner of his eyes matched by the brackets on either side of his mouth. His features were so familiar from all those evenings on the sofa laughing along with his modest self-deprecating comments that she had to remind herself that he was a stranger to her. Then there was also the fact that, much as she'd told herself not to have any expectations, she hadn't been able to resist the occasional fantasy regarding what would happen on the island. She'd imagined that, as she met each challenge with grit and determination, Nick's admiration for her would grow and one night as they were gazing into the fire he'd suggest that just because their adventure was coming to an end didn't mean their friendship had to.

"I've shared more with you in two weeks," he'd say, "than with people I've known my whole life." And then maybe he'd take her hand in his and lean towards her...

Except that now he thought she was some sort of hysterical bimbo.

Great start.

She suddenly remembered Kenny's camera and she

turned her attention back to Lois, hoping Kenny hadn't caught her looking too moony.

Lois was still talking. "The first show goes out in two days, on Friday, and it's going to be one hour a night every night after that, made up of edits from the handhelds, the Island Eyes and the confession cam. That's what I'll be spending my days doing, just in case you think I'm going to be out there drinking piña coladas on deck while you're scrounging for grubs and berries here."

They all smiled dutifully.

Lois came over to Jessie and handed her something that looked like a button on a shoelace. "Here, wear this around your neck." She showed her a small black box. "This is the transmitter. Just clip it onto your dress or underwear or whatever. I want you all miked-up all the time, though please remember to take them off when you go in the water. Say something, Jess."

"I prefer to be called Jessie, not Jess."

"Got it," said Kenny, tapping his headphones.

"Good," said Lois. "Don't worry, you'll soon forget you have it on. Now, I think that's it. I'll be coming back and forth from the yacht anyway to iron out any wrinkles as they occur. Kenny will stop filming in the evenings and start up again at 7:00 a.m. so you'll have the nights to yourself." She treated them to another feline smile. "Apart from the Island Eyes, of course. Are there any questions?"

"So we haven't really started yet?" asked Jessie. "I mean, will that stuff in the water be used?"

"We'll use whatever's good," said Lois disingenuously. "So, welcome to your new home away from home and good luck to all of you."

Silence followed and they all looked at each other until Lois made shooing gestures. "Go," she said impatiently. "That's it."

Nick took a step towards Jessie and held out his hand. "I'm Nick Garrett," he said. "Welcome to the island."

"Jessie Banks." Their eyes met as she introduced herself but she looked away quickly, infuriated to feel herself blushing.

"You've met the others?"

Jessie nodded, smiling. If Nick wanted to pretend that that little incident in the water had never happened, she could go along with that.

"Okay then," said Nick, turning to Malcolm and Cindi. "Why don't we go and show Jessie what we've done so far?"

Jessie let the others go ahead of her and she turned hurriedly to Lois and Kenny.

"I'm sorry to have to ask," she said, "but I really could use a drink of water."

Lois pointed at Nick. "Ask him," she mouthed. "We're not here."

Jessie looked at Nick's retreating back and muttered an oath under her breath.

"For the record," came Kenny's calm voice behind her, "the microphone you're wearing is very strong."

Jessie blushed again and started up the beach after Nick.

"I WAS JUST WONDERING—"

"Malcolm constructed the second eave of his shelter by himself," said Nick. "He's a fast learner."

"That's great," said Jessie. Her throat was getting more parched by the minute but the others weren't giving her any opportunity to broach the subject. They were too eager to show her the shelters they'd built the night before.

Jessie nodded politely as Malcolm extolled the virtues of vegetation as an insulating material but her eyes were darting around, trying to locate the supplies.

How rude is this, she thought, inviting someone to your

home and not offering them a drink? Even if the home in question is only a smoldering fire and three V-shaped tents made out of sticks and grass.

Her disenchantment must have showed on her face.

"I hope you're not getting cold feet," Nick teased her. "I had to give a pep-talk to the others last night and I'm going to tell you the same thing now. The competition and the prize money, that's only a small part of our stay here. Despite what my producer might think, this is not a game show. It's going to be the real thing. A lot of my viewers are no strangers to survival situations themselves and I'm not going to cheat them by taking shortcuts. We've come onto this island with no supplies and we won't be getting any help. It's going to be up to us."

"Speaking of supplies," Jessie cut in. "I was wondering if I could get a drink of water. I got salt in my throat and it's also much hotter here than I'm used to."

"That's a good idea," said Nick. "Cindi, Malcolm, let's see if you remember what to do. What's the first step of purifying water?"

"Filter it," gushed Malcolm.

"Right, and what do you do then?" Nick looked at Cindi who was fiddling with the skirt of her uniform.

"Is it heating it?" She squinted. "I forget."

Nick tsked. "Okay, Malcolm can show you. Get to work."

Today maybe, thought Jessie. Her dress was beginning to dry in the sun and she was longing to have a look around the island. The beach stretched enticingly in either direction and she could see palm trees swaying in the distance. But she couldn't concentrate on any of it when her mouth felt like it had an inbuilt dehumidifier. She moved her tongue, trying to dredge up some saliva.

"What are you doing?" asked Nick.

Jessie stopped masticating. "Nothing," she said vehemently before she realized he was talking to the others. She coughed and mimicked his look of concerned curiosity.

"We're boiling water," Malcolm said hesitantly.

Nick walked over and kicked apart the embers of the fire. "I lit this fire," he pointed out. "I want to see if you can do it."

Another milligram of Jessie's patience slipped away.

"So we need tinder materials," said Malcolm enthusiastically. "And something to produce friction."

"That's good," said Nick. "I hope you're paying attention Cindi, I'll expect you to do it next time."

Cindi gave him a flirtatious grin. "I pay attention to everything you say, Nick."

"Apparently not," he retorted playfully.

Jessie fiddled with a strand of her hair, considering the possibility that she might actually shrivel up and die of dehydration, right there on television.

She watched with mounting despair as Malcolm fumbled with a stick and a piece of bark.

"No," he complained to Cindi, "you have to use the dry moss first. Try and crumble it up into smaller pieces and hold it over to the side."

"You're supposed to move the stick faster," nagged Cindi in return. "It has to smolder."

"On a scale of one to ten," Jessie said conversationally, "how bad would it be to drink salt water?"

Nick smiled at her, evidently under the impression that she was joking. "About a five. It wouldn't kill you but it wouldn't do anything for your thirst, just make you feel worse."

"Worse than I do now," murmured Jessie. "Imagine." Her throat was so dry that she couldn't even swallow.

Another five minutes passed and Nick hunkered down to help out.

Jessie looked out to sea, at the yacht bobbing gracefully in the distance. She glanced at Kenny who was quietly filming them. She looked down to the shore, where Lois was yapping on a walkie-talkie.

She silently counted to ten and then opened her purse and took out the lipstick.

Nick paused in his efforts and looked up at her in disbelief. "Making sure you look good for the cameras?"

Jessie didn't answer. She took the top off the lipstick and rolled it up, catching the matches as they emerged. She held one out to Nick.

"Here, tough guy, let's get this show on the road."

She couldn't help smirking as his eyes widened in surprise.

Malcolm barked a laugh. "Where'd you get those?"

Jessie held up her sparkly evening bag and felt a glow of satisfaction as a small smile quirked the corners of Nick's mouth. She rolled the matches back into the lipstick and tucked it away in her purse, then met Nick's eyes.

"Look," she cajoled, waving the match, "next time you can light it from scratch but I really need a drink, right now."

The laughter lines around Nick's eyes deepened. He took the match and started to scrape the waterproofing wax off it.

"Are you going to keep calling me that?" he said in an undertone.

"What?"

"Tough guy," he muttered.

He looked vaguely uncomfortable, which Jessie found endearing. "I'm not sure," she teased. "I'm kind of getting used to it."

Nick struck the match and Jessie gave a cheer as the small bundle of tinder lit into flames.

"HI, EVERYONE! Uh...is this on? Well, I'm going to assume that red light means it is." Jessie got comfortable in the seat and beamed at the camera.

"Welcome to Castaway Island and this, my very first broadcast. I have to say that it's quite strange to be talking into a camera like this but I'm sure I'll get used to it." She waved cheerfully. "A big hi to all my friends back home in Iowa. Look, I made it! Martha and Sophie, I hope you're being nice to everyone at work and hello to all the regulars at Fairbury Library. Janice, you'd better have one of your apple pies ready for me when I come home, something tells me I'll have quite an appetite. Marty, thanks again for house-sitting and feeding Toby and I'd better have both a house and a dog when I come back. No wild parties, I mean it."

Jessie paused and subconsciously folded her arms. "And Tom, hi. Thanks for seeing me off at the airport. Uh...I haven't thought...that is to say...what I mean is I'll see you when I get back."

She looked down, trying to recover her train of thought and quickly found something else that bore mentioning. "Ah yes, my dress. Well, what do you think? Pretty glamorous, eh? It's what every fashion-conscious castaway is wearing this season." She made a wry face. "Don't know if you've seen what the others are wearing, but I think I drew the short straw. I might have to steal Malcolm's jacket while he's sleeping." She laughed. "Don't worry Debs, I'm only kidding. I'm sure that neither Cindi or I will be doing anything to your husband while he's sleeping."

Jessie paused, thinking. She wanted to make a joke about how the other contestants deserved the money so much more than her, but she was afraid that the audience might take her seriously. There was no point sabotaging herself from the start.

She searched the sides of the hut for inspiration. "Oh, jeepers, I almost forgot." She laughed at the camera. "And all you gals out there are probably yelling at me to get to the good stuff. Well, Nick Garrett is currently getting some food together for our dinner, which I'm really looking forward to. I'm starving." Her eyes twinkled playfully. "But at least I'm not thirsty anymore. But I will warn you now that there will be a preponderance of shots of me drinking water. It is hot, hot, hot here. I guess that's what you get when you come to the Tropics." She looked up at the thatched ceiling. "Although, it's not so bad in here. This shade is nice."

Then she realized she was rambling and she looked back at the unblinking eye with the red light underneath it. "Where was I? Oh, yes, Nick's making dinner." She hesitated and then resolved not to let the silly misunderstandings cloud her judgment. It was much too soon to be saying things that she could regret. "So, I'm here to tell you that he is just as handsome and friendly in real life as he is on TV. A little overeager in some cases," she couldn't help adding, "but that's hardly a crime." Her mouth curved cheekily. "He's very good at lighting fires."

She rushed on. "And later, I'm really looking forward to exploring the island." Her eyes lit up. "This place is so amazing. You should see the—" She broke off, laughing. "Hang on, you are seeing it. Okay, I think I must be getting delirious from hunger, I'd better go and see what's cooking."

She put a hand to her hair, thinking again of her friends. "I was in the water so I might look a bit bedraggled but I'm feeling good so don't worry about me...just keep watching this space! Uh...that's it, bye. Over and out."

She waited a moment to see if the red light went out but it didn't so eventually she just got up and left the hut.

"NO WAY," SAID CINDI. "It's just not going to happen."

Kenny panned the camera down slowly to zoom in on the squirming, fat, beetle grubs and then up again to record the contestants' expressions of repulsion.

"It's okay, I am going to cook them," Nick said.

Cindi shook her head. "I don't care. I am not eating those. They're disgusting. They even smell bad."

Malcolm rubbed his hands together. "Sorry, Cindi, but if that's your attitude, you're going to be easy to beat. I have no problem with eating grubs."

"Wait a minute," said Cindi in outrage. "We haven't started the challenges yet, have we? I thought we were starting tomorrow."

Nick was cutting up some sweet potatoes and he paused to look at Cindi.

"Why?" he smiled. "Would you eat them if it was part of a challenge?"

Cindi jutted out her chin. "Of course."

Nick nodded thoughtfully and went back to work. "I'll keep that in mind."

Cindi gave Jessie a look of dread, making Jessie laugh. She looked at Nick who put the potatoes in a large tin of water and started to cook them over the fire.

"Where did you get that?" she asked suspiciously, pointing at the tin. "I thought we were surviving from scratch here."

Nick looked up, pleased. "We went beachcombing yesterday. Managed to find ourselves some treasure."

"Treasure?" Jessie smiled, playing along. "Like Spanish doubloons?"

Nick pointed out towards the west. "Now that you mention it, there have been ships wrecked on the coral reefs out there so it's not unknown for the odd coin to be found on islands in these parts." He put up a hand to forestall her excitement. "But I was actually talking about treasure of a different kind. Like this, which as far as I can tell is an old paint tin. Don't ask me how it got here, maybe someone was touching up the paint job on their boat. Anyway, to us, it's a cooking pot." He looked up at Malcolm. "Want to tell her what else we got?"

Malcolm didn't hesitate. "A rope. About ten feet long. And not as rotted as it seemed at first."

"Cindi?" said Nick.

"Don't tell me," Cindi said eagerly. "I know this." She scrunched her nose up prettily before sitting up straight with excitement. "Ooh, I've got it. Two bottles. So now we've got something to store our clean water in and to drink out of."

"And to send SOS messages in," commented Jessie, earning herself a grin from Nick.

"And we got some different-sized shells," Nick added, handing them around. "Which we can use as bowls and spoons."

They took their eating utensils and then watched with quiet curiosity as Nick whittled at a thin stick, scraping off the bark and sharpening one end to a point. He picked up one of the unappetizing white grubs and, without ceremony, speared it upon a stick.

"Eeeouw," howled Cindi, flinging her hands over her face.

Jessie couldn't help looking away as well. Malcolm kept watching as Nick impaled the remaining grubs, but his face was a few shades paler by the end.

Nick grinned cheerfully at their reactions and held the beetle-grub kebab over the fire while he stirred the sweet potatoes.

He gave Malcolm the job of straining the potatoes and dishing them out, while he concentrated on cooking the grubs evenly. They crackled as they gradually turned golden and crispy.

Unbelievably, Jessie's mouth was watering.

They all made short work of the potatoes and then Nick asked for a volunteer.

"I will!" said Malcolm.

"Hold on a second," said Nick, his eyes glinting mischievously. "Whatever happened to 'ladies first'?"

"Very funny," said Cindi, grimacing. "Forget it."

Nick raised his eyebrows at Jessie and she caught her bottom lip between her teeth.

"Okay," she whispered, smiling excitedly at her own daring.

Nick held out the stick and Jessie hesitated for a second, then she reached out and plucked off a grub, closing her eyes as she popped it into her mouth.

It was succulent and sweet, like a ball of crackling pork.

Jessie opened her eyes as she chewed it. "This is delicious," she said. She looked at Cindi. "Seriously. You should try one."

Cindi put up her hands. "No offence, but I just met you and, frankly, I don't believe you."

Poor Malcolm was almost quivering with the desire to display his grit, so Nick took pity on him and handed him the stick. Malcolm removed a grub and then paused, a frown shadowing his round face.

"Are these high in cholesterol?"

JESSIE SMOTHERED ANOTHER yawn as she watched the dancing flames. She'd thought she might go exploring after dinner but in the end she just didn't feel like moving from the fireside.

It was her first chance to really think about what she'd let herself in for. Her expectations and hypotheses had been inadequate preparation. In her imagination the other contestants had been mere ciphers, just background figures in Jessie's adventure with Nick Garrett. A few short hours with them had cured her of that misconception. They were real people, with their own personalities and their own agendas.

Throughout dinner and afterwards, Jessie had been quietly studying them, trying to work out why they had been picked out of the thousands of people who had entered the competition.

Malcolm was so innocuous and eager to please that Jessie had come to the conclusion that he was there simply because he was the embodiment of Everyman. He was ordinary and human and easy to identify with.

And Cindi was obviously the sassy, worldly, city girl—a part she seemed more than happy to play.

But if they were dealing with stereotypes, what role had Jessie been drafted for?

She raised her eyes from the fire and stole a quick glance at Nick. He was whittling efficiently at some sticks, creating rudimentary forks and spoons out of pieces of wood. Jessie looked down again, grappling with her thoughts.

To her dismay, the mild crush she had on Nick Garrett, TV personality, had transferred itself directly onto Nick Garrett, actual person. Jessie had been prepared to be somewhat awed and starstruck on meeting him at first but she'd presumed it would only be a temporary imbalance. Unfortunately, there was no sign of it dissipating. She was trying to act normal but her heart still took on an erratic beat whenever their eyes met, and her capacity for putting together sentences, which she'd always taken for granted, seemed to desert her whenever he was around.

It was especially horrible because it was just so clichéd. He had all the ingredients for a male fantasy figure. His features weren't perfect but somehow they added up to a face that was warm and welcoming. His eyes were very clear and intelligent and his mouth always seemed to be on the verge of a smile, even when things were going from bad to worse, as they occasionally did on his show. He was friendly, easy-going and genuine and Jessie found herself utterly tongue-tied in his presence.

Her only consolation was that she didn't think it was showing.

Up until now.

Now that she was alone with him, things were becoming strained. Malcolm had gone off eagerly to do his time with the confession camera and, when the dinghy had come to pick up Kenny for the night, Cindi had volunteered to walk him down to the shore—and Jessie still wasn't sure what *that* was about.

Jessie and Nick hadn't talked for over ten minutes and while Nick seemed unperturbed by the silence Jessie was desperately searching for something to say. She kept coming up with lighthearted conversation topics and then discarding them because they seemed trite or forced and the more time that passed the more pressured she felt. She'd been so glad when the others had left them alone and now she was just praying for their return. A movement caught her eye and she looked up to see Nick holding up the spoons.

"No more eating with shells," he said cheerfully.

"Yes," said Jessie. There was a painful pause and then she added, "Indeed." She smiled inanely and looked out towards the shore. She could see Cindi chatting to Kenny and the crewman who had come to collect him. What was that girl up to?

Jessie looked back at Nick, realizing in a rush that there *was* something that needed to be said.

"Uh, look, I'm sorry I yelled at you earlier, when I came ashore. I know you were only trying to help."

Nick glanced up. "That's okay. I'm sorry I tried to save your life."

Jessie blinked. She hadn't expected sarcasm.

Nick put his hand to his head and let out a low laugh. "No, wait a minute, that came out wrong."

Jessie smiled, feeling an odd surge of affection at his embarrassment.

"I really didn't mean that the way it sounded," he went on. "I promise. I'm sorry, too. Sorry that we got off on the wrong foot."

"I can see how easily you might have thought I was in trouble," Jessie said generously. "You were right to try and save me. Better safe than sorry."

He shook his head in mock regret. "I don't know. At the time I thought you were going to start whacking me with your bag. I was about to throw you back in."

Jessie laughed.

"Of course, now I know why you were so anxious to rescue that bag," said Nick. Jessie nodded smugly, at last beginning to feel the possibility that she might make friends with Nick.

"I hope Lois doesn't get too mad," she said.

Nick tilted his head quizzically and then she saw comprehension dawn on his features.

"You smuggled those onshore," he said.

Jessie nodded, pleased by Nick's obvious admiration. She didn't even notice Cindi's return.

"What are you looking so happy about?" said Cindi.

Jessie flushed. "What? What do you mean?"

"Relax," said Cindi, "I was just asking." She sat down on the log next to Nick and leaned over to nudge him playfully with her shoulder. "I'm afraid that I might have interrupted a little tête-à-tête."

Jessie wanted to go over and push Cindi off the log. Nothing sophisticated, just push her so she went ass over teakettle onto the sand. She didn't know if it was deliberate or not but Cindi was exhibiting a real knack for dissolving any burgeoning friendship that Nick and Jessie managed to achieve and embarrassing them back into self-conscious formality. Or maybe it was just Jessie she was embarrassing.

"Anybody mind if I hit the hay?" said Malcolm, joining them at the fire and evidently not noticing any strain in the atmosphere. "I'm exhausted again and I don't even know why. It's not like we even did that much today."

"It'll take time for your bodies to get used to the heat," said Nick. "Just wait until tomorrow, you'll really find out what tiredness is about." He laughed at their expressions. "It's a good idea for us all to get some rest."

They got to their feet, stretching and yawning in the mild night air.

Cindi looked at Jessie in consternation. "Where are you sleeping, Jessie?"

Jessie looked around in dismay. She hadn't even thought about it. Had they expected her to build a shelter? Why hadn't anyone said anything?

"She's sleeping with me," Nick said casually.

Jessie looked at him and then let out a laugh. "Oops," she giggled. "Did you hear what you said? Another slip of the tongue."

He looked at her blankly. "No. I meant it."

Jessie swallowed. "Excuse me?"

"Sorry, I should have explained sooner. You're going to share my shelter tonight. There's too much risk that you'll get cold overnight on your own and if I share out my clothes it'll just leave us both underdressed. This is the only way to do it until we've had a chance to scavenge something to make clothes out of."

He gave her a frank smile. "I promise I'm not trying to take advantage of you, it's just a survival tactic. If you get cold you won't be able to sleep and you'll be irritable tomorrow." His eyes grew playful. "You might try and attack me with your bag."

Jessie returned his smile and offered a suggestion. "Maybe I should bunk down with Cindi instead."

"Sorry," said Nick. "I'm under instructions from Lois. Since you're all competing she wants to keep you separated."

Jessie nodded, keeping her face impassive. Trust Lois. Even though Kenny was gone, Jessie had no doubts that their sleeping arrangements were going to be caught on one of the Island Eyes. The woman knew how to make good television.

Jessie glanced up at the nearby trees, wondering if there was a camera focused on her right now and hoping that her indifferent expression was fooling it. She might be feigning resignation with Lois's decision but inside she was jittering with nervous excitement at the thought of sharing a bed with Nick.

Cindi was evidently thinking along the same lines.

"Well, aren't you the fast mover, girl," she said with an outrageous grin. "I guess you knew exactly what you were doing when you wore that dress." Cindi giggled as if she was only kidding around, but Jessie's face flamed regardless.

"It's not...I didn't plan on..."

"It's about survival," said Nick, unruffled. "Nothing more."

"Survival of the species," said Cindi in an undertone to Jessie. "It wouldn't surprise me if Nick's planning a little propagation. Lucky you."

"Oh, right," Jessie whispered back. "Like we could do anything without you and Malcolm hearing it."

Cindi raised an eyebrow. "So you *have* been thinking about it."

Jessie shook her head, but Cindi just winked at her. "Sleep tight," she said as she sauntered off to her own shelter.

"Okay, you too," said Jessie with forced brightness. "See you in the morning Malcolm."

"Yup," he said. "Good night." Malcolm obviously didn't intend to be as blunt as Cindi but he didn't have to be. Jessie could see the inevitable speculation in his eyes.

Jessie winced and then she followed Nick over to his shelter, trying to shake the feeling that she was the chosen concubine.

"Are you tired?" asked Nick conversationally.

She nodded, realizing that the weakness in her legs needn't necessarily be attributed to the fact that she was about to bed down with Nick Garrett.

She was just tired, that was it.

Her eyes widened in alarm as Nick unbuttoned his shirt. He took it off and then pulled his T-shirt over his head in one fluid motion.

Jessie couldn't tear her gaze away from Nick's chest, naked except for the microphone around his neck. She didn't know what to do. Had she been completely wrong about him? About this show? Was she expected to have sex with him after all? On camera?

"Here," said Nick, handing her his T-shirt. "Put this on." He put his shirt back on and bent to untie his boots. "I'll give you my socks as well, they should be some help."

Jessie, mortified by her assumptions and touched by his consideration, slipped the T-shirt over her head. It smelt of him and she wrapped her arms around herself as she felt the lingering warmth of him seep into her skin.

Nick gave her his socks and then covered his microphone, indicating she should do the same. Jessie wrapped her hand around the microphone and stared at his face, shadowed in the moonlit night.

"I just wanted to tell you that you don't have to worry about...I mean, what Lois said earlier about the sexual tension...that's not something you have to worry about."

Jessie felt her chest constrict and she was glad of the darkness. "Oh, gosh," she fumbled, "you neither. I mean, you don't have to worry. Of course not."

He nodded and smiled. "Come on, let's get some sleep. Big day tomorrow." He tilted up the roof of the shelter so Jessie could lie down and then he arranged himself next to her, lowering the roof above them.

The bed was too narrow to allow any space between them and anyway, Nick seemed devoid of any self-consciousness as he slid one hand under her neck and curved his arm protectively around her. He was lying on his back and Jessie found herself nestled in the crook of his arm, her back snuggled warmly against his side. She could feel the steady rise and fall of his chest and she made an effort to slow her own breathing, certain that he could feel her heart thudding like a piston. Her gaze dropped to Nick's arm and she could see the golden hairs glinting in the tiny rays of moonlight that seeped through the roof branches. She could imagine the salt on his skin and wondered how he'd react if she just tilted her head down and licked it.

She closed her eyes. A few moments passed and then she decided that she didn't care if the others were less than ten feet away. She was in bed with Nick Garrett and she was going to make the most of it. She rose up and turned over in the bed. She looked down at Nick who was watching her with dark eyes and she moved over until she was straddling his lap. She peeled off the T-shirt and then slowly, tantalizingly, dropped first one strap and then the other until her breasts were bared to his gaze.

Nick's reaction was immediate and passionate and probably would have done him proud had he been aware of it. Jessie had already succumbed to sleep and her flickering eyelids were the only evidence that such a shameless seduction was taking place.

3

NICK WAS WOKEN by the bright sun shining through the pin-hole gaps in the leaves of the shelter. The air was comfortably warm and he could hear birdsong and the rhythmic crash of the waves on the shore.

He yawned and looked down at the head that was resting in the crook of his shoulder. He could see the sweep of Jessie's brows and her chestnut hair fell in a thick cascade over his arm. She stirred in her sleep and her mouth parted to emit a soft snore.

Nick smiled, remembering how quickly she'd fallen asleep the night before. He'd deepened his breathing as soon as they lay down, hoping to put her at ease by making her think he was already asleep. He hadn't been sure what kind of reaction to expect to the revelation that they were sharing a bed but the way she just lay down next to him without making any sort of fuss about it had impressed him.

Truth be told, his overall impression of her was a good one. She seemed to have a lot of spirit and he liked the determined glint that had sparked in her eye when it came time to eat the beetle grubs.

Nick had been unenthusiastic about this castaway competition from the start. He was used to working on his own—just him and the elements—and he had tried doggedly to disenchant Lois of the idea. But she had remained resolute and while Nick knew that she couldn't fire him she did have the power to thwart or curtail his future projects. Working *with* Lois was a particular kind of torture, working *against* her didn't even bear thinking about.

So it had never really been a matter of "if," but "when."

Of course now that he was in it, he had to admit that he was intrigued by what was going to happen. In his show he reminded viewers over and over again that psychology played a vital part in survival. In extreme circumstances a strong mind could make a weak body do impossible things. But the reverse was also true. When the mind gave up, the body followed.

The fascination of watching random people under pressure was irresistible. Who'll crack, who'll turn nasty, who'll come through with their integrity intact, who'll surprise?

Nick also knew that when a group of people found themselves in a genuinely life-threatening situation it was always only a matter of time before the instinct for self-preservation caused rifts and betrayals. However, the castaways with Nick were obviously in no real danger of starving to death. And so, the money prize had been introduced to provide the necessary incentive to selfishness and backstabbing.

How long before they stopped working together?

Nick smiled to himself as his thoughts meandered. Lois had done a good job of picking the finalists. Nick knew that hopeful contestants had sent in a biography and an essay detailing their most impressive survival experience to date but he had never gotten to see these. Neither had Lois told him anything about the eventual finalists. Her idea was that it would make it more interesting for him to be in the dark about these strangers that he was stranded with.

He'd had little more than perfunctory conversations with them so far. He knew that Cindi was a bartender in New York—"By which I mean, I admit it, I'm an actress. Between jobs, you know?"—and that Malcolm was some sort of accountant—"Figures and statistics, I won't bore you with it."

And his impression of Jessie? Only fleeting so far but he liked her. What was it she'd called him? Tough guy. It should have annoyed him but there was something about the way she said it, so casually and without a hint of flirtation, that made it sort of charming.

Out of the corner of his eye he glimpsed movement at the opening of the shelter and he tilted his head up to see Kenny's camera trained on them.

Nick let out a quiet chuckle. "Morning. How about giving us a minute to wake up?"

Kenny lifted a hand in greeting but didn't move away as Jessie started to stir. She let out a sigh and her eyelids fluttered open. She looked blankly at Nick for a moment, blinking, until a smile of recognition curved her lips.

Nick instinctively returned the smile. "Morning."

"Yeah...hi," mumbled Jessie, putting a hand up to brush some strands of hair back from her face. She rubbed her eyes and blinked a few more times, looking around blearily as if getting her bearings.

She raised herself onto one elbow and, catching sight of Kenny, let out a laughing groan and turned away from him, hiding her face.

The next moment Jessie burst through the top of the shelter, shrieking at the top of her lungs.

Nick watched, stunned, as her head disappeared through the hole in the roof and he heard her exclaim to Kenny, "Did you see that? It's enormous!"

Nick winced. He had hoped that if she did notice the bulge in his trousers that she would at least have had the diplomacy not to mention it. Her comments, flattering though they were, were the last thing he'd expected or wanted. What was the matter with her?

He looked down just in time to see a gecko lizard slithering off the bed, its long tail flickering as it scuttled out of the hut.

Nick got up, running his hand through his hair and stretched as he emerged from the shelter. He smiled when he saw Jessie watching fearfully from a distance.

"It's okay," he said, raising his hands in a gesture of triumph. "I have vanquished the monster."

"What the heck was it?"

"It was just a gecko lizard."

"A lizard?" said Jessie. "Are you kidding me? Lizards are small and cute. That was as big as a dog."

Nick offered the camera a skeptical look. "More like a cat really."

"It was sleeping on top of us!"

"Yeah," said Nick. "They like the warmth. And maybe the companionship, who knows?"

"Great. I hope the two of you will be very happy together. Don't forget to invite me to the wedding."

"Look," said Nick reasonably. "There's no need to be scared. They're vegetarians, harmless really."

He watched as a flush rose on Jessie's cheeks. She was obviously considering how her reaction had looked on camera.

"I wasn't scared," she explained. "I just got a fright. I wasn't expecting to wake up next to a lizard."

"I'll take that as a compliment," quipped Nick.

He was pleased to see Jessie smile sheepishly. She pressed her hand to her chest as if calming a racing heart.

"Phew," she breathed. "And to think that I was worried about being able to wake up properly without my morning cup of coffee."

Nick laughed. As startling as it had been, at least the incident obliterated any awkwardness that might have hung over them waking up together.

Then he looked over at Cindi and Malcolm, who had

emerged from their respective shelters with the same shocked expression.

Of course, Jessie's shriek *was* still going to take some explaining.

"I WAS NOT TRYING TO molest her," said Nick for the fourth time. "Will you please stop saying that I was." He indicated the trees. "We are on camera, you know."

Cindi made the unconvinced and uncaring face of a cop writing up a ticket. "I'm just saying it was an awful big yell to have been caused by such a little thing."

"It wasn't little," grumbled Jessie. "It was huge. It was a mutant lizard. You'd have screamed, too."

Cindi waved a dismissive hand. "I'm not really phobic about reptiles."

"Neither am I," argued Jessie hotly, her voice heading for the top end of the scales again.

Malcolm interrupted the squabble. "I have a phobia of—"

Silence, punctuated by the hiss of simmering water, followed.

"Of?" prompted Nick.

Malcolm sank his head into his neck and looked unhappy. "I don't want to say."

Nick regarded him for a moment, then smiled in approving comprehension. "You think I'll use it against you."

Malcolm nodded, miserable with the strain of defying his hero.

"I'm phobic about pizza," said Cindi with a hopeful expression. "Please don't make me eat pizza, I'll freak out."

"Only two days and already you're dreaming about pizza?" said Nick in a disappointed voice.

Jessie spoke up. "I, too, find it hard to believe that the thrill of sweet potatoes would ever wear off, having had them for both dinner and breakfast already."

"Okay," surrendered Nick. "Don't worry. Our diet will become more varied. I saw some banana trees on the other side of the island and we'll find lots of papaya bushes inland. And of course we'll be catching fish. Best of all though, when I got those delicious potatoes I noticed that there was evidence of damage around the stems and leaves."

"From mutant lizards," guessed Jessie.

"Even better," grinned Nick. "From wild pigs."

Jessie raised a dubious eyebrow. "And that's good, how?"

Malcolm interrupted eagerly. "It's great. We can hunt them and have a roast."

"*You* can hunt them," clarified Jessie.

Malcolm turned to Nick. "Can I?" he said, like a child asking permission to run downstairs on Christmas morning.

"Sure," said Nick. He liked that Malcolm's enthusiasm was unfettered by his manifest ineptitude.

Jessie lifted her face to the sun and then took off the T-shirt that Nick had given her, handing it back to him with a smile.

"It's so warm already," she said. "I'll definitely need a swim later." She rustled in her sparkly evening bag and drew out a thin tube of sunscreen, applying some to her face before offering it to the others.

"That's okay," said Nick. "My skin is used to the outdoors."

Cindi also demurred, explaining that she and the sun-bed were old friends.

"No tan lines," she added provocatively.

Nick watched Malcolm keeping his gaze fixed firmly on the ground and then he looked at Jessie. She was smiling blandly as she held the sunscreen out to Malcolm but her foot was jiggling. With impatience, or annoyance at Cindi?

Malcolm eventually glanced up and noticed Jessie's offering. He hesitated, as if he wanted to be macho and refuse, but then he took it and slicked some quickly over his nose.

Nick let his eyes drift to the middle distance again, before anyone realized they'd been observed.

The growl of an engine broke the morning stillness and they all looked out to the shore and slowly got to their feet as they saw the motorboat pulling up.

"Yoo-hoo!" Lois called as she came trotting up the sand towards them. Her eyes were hidden behind dark sunglasses but her mouth was curved in a broad smile.

"Success!" she exclaimed, raising her hands in excitement. "Just wait until you hear."

Whoa, thought Nick, looks like someone around here has had their morning coffee.

Her hands gesticulating madly to emphasize her words, Lois spoke to the group assembled. "We played the tapes for our test audience and, get this, Jessie, they *loved* you. I'm not kidding, they thought you were really fresh and feisty and then you bowled them over with how nice you were on the confession cam. Good work!"

Nick looked at Jessie. Her mouth was gaping in surprise. "Looks like you're a natural," he said encouragingly.

Lois turned her attention to Nick. "I know," she said happily. "I can't believe it. The audience even gave you some stick for rescuing her when she so obviously didn't need it."

Nick's brow creased slightly. "What?"

Lois nodded. "Yeah, isn't it cute? She's become a sort of heroine of the people. They love her indomitable spirit and her cheeky talk-back attitude."

It was Jessie's turn to look nonplussed. "My what?"

Lois ignored her. "It's better than I'd dared to hope," she said, gazing dreamily out over the ocean. Her eyes flicked back to Jessie's. "I'm even going to let you keep your bag of tricks." She wagged her finger. "Bold girl. I don't know how you thought you'd get away with smuggling."

"That'll teach you to mess with the gestapo," muttered Cindi.

Lois shifted her laser stare. "Having a talk-back attitude with *me* isn't going to earn you any points, take my word for it." She flicked through the pages on her clipboard. "But I will tell you that you've got a lot of admirers, too. We're hearing very complimentary things about your looks. General consensus, you're quite a beauty."

Cindi smiled and lowered her eyes modestly but Nick noticed that she didn't exactly blush.

"What about me?" asked Malcolm.

"Er, yes, they like you, too," was Lois's lukewarm response. "Anyway," she went on, brightening, "everyone's really looking forward to seeing how real-life people cope with life-and-death situations. They can't wait to see you thrown into the fray. So, Nick, what have you got planned for us?"

"I thought that the first thing we should do is see how they fare at catching some fish."

"Fishing," said Lois, nodding in a thoughtful manner. "Right. Okay, why don't you just get a gun and shoot me right now? Fishing's the most boring thing I've ever heard. People don't want to see fishing. They want to see these three put to the test. Challenged. Thrust into the action. They want to see a struggle." She caught Jessie's anxious expression. "Because they believe in you," she reassured her, oozing sincerity. "They think you're all just great. They identify with you and they really want to see how an ordinary person copes with the reality of life-or-death survival." Lois framed her hands in the air as if sketching a blurb on a movie poster. "What they lack in experience they make up for in pluck and sheer grit."

Nick stole a look at Lois's victims. The two women wore

doubtful expressions but Malcolm's eyes were shining with evangelical zeal.

Lois raced on. "So we can have fishing and building rafts and all that, sure, but I'm thinking it'd be good if these things were somehow, I dunno, dangerous as well." She looked speculative. "Are there alligators in these waters?"

"Wait a minute," gasped Jessie. "I thought this was going to be about ordinary, practical survival. I didn't come here for—"

"Look," interrupted Lois brusquely, "you watch the show, right? So you've got a fighting chance. Anyway, it's not important that you succeed. What matters is that we get to see you try. Even if you fall flat on your face it'll still be great television and Nick will always be there to save the day."

Nick decided it was time to step in. "There are no alligators in these waters, Lois, you know that, and even if there were, nobody here would be in any danger from them, I'd make sure of that. And furthermore," he went on firmly, "fishing is life-or-death, we have to eat. So that's what we're going to do." He turned to the others who were looking at him with varying degrees of gratitude and disappointment. "Now, if you watch the show, you should have some idea of what to do." He took three bound coils of fishing line from his pocket and handed them around. "This is all I'm going to give you. You can go wherever you want and use whatever method you like and the first one to bring back a fish wins, simple as that."

"Oh, wow," said Malcolm, bounding off as if fired from a catapult, "I can do this."

"Jessie?" asked Nick. "You ready?"

"Absolutely," she said eagerly. "I know what to do. I watch the show every week. I'm a big fan."

She walked off briskly and Nick turned to Cindi who was making an apologetic face.

"I'll get you started," said Nick, putting a hand on her elbow and leading her towards the shore.

It was safer than staying with Lois.

"I WATCH THE SHOW every week," sneered Jessie. "I'm a big fan." She cringed as another wave of embarrassment engulfed her. Could she possibly have been more ingratiating? She didn't think so.

She tried telling herself to concentrate on the task at hand but there really wasn't anything left for her to do. She'd put together a very respectable fishing rod in about half an hour. She'd made a lure out of a small gull feather and some sequins torn off her bag, tied together with a thread from the hem of her dress. The hook had taken longer but she'd eventually managed to splice two sharp slivers of wood together and attach them to the end of the line that Nick had supplied.

She was sitting on the end of a long promontory that jutted straight out into the sea. Her feet were dangling a few yards above the water which was so clear that she could see the sand and plant-life under the surface and she even caught the occasional glimpse of a fish as it shimmered by. Gulls wheeled overhead and sometimes one would plunge into the sea, then flap upwards with a wriggling fish clamped in its beak.

Her position also gave her a clear view of what the others were doing. Malcolm was at the other end of the beach and had left his fishing rod propped upright in the sand, while he seemed to be making something that was either a kitchen cabinet or an oddly shaped raft. Kenny was with him, recording the whole thing.

In the middle of the beach were Nick and Cindi. They were thigh-deep in the lapping waves and Nick was apparently teaching Cindi how to cast the line. Except that, even after an hour Cindi still didn't seem to be getting the hang of it. She had taken off her chambermaid's uniform and was now standing in her bra and panties, which Jessie could see, even from a distance, were hot pink. She watched as Cindi's head tilted backwards as she laughed at something that Nick had said.

Jessie looked back at her fishing rod and gave it a desultory jiggle. She couldn't stop brooding over what she'd said to Nick and the only distraction from the embarrassment was finding another new scratch or bite from the night before. The bed had been comfortable enough but when all was said and done it had still been a bed of twigs and foliage. She picked at her nails, trying to dislodge some of the dirt from under them. She just had a general feeling of grubbiness. She could feel the sand in her hair and the sticks that Nick had encouraged them to chew that morning proved a poor replacement for teeth that had been reared on soft bristles and fluoride. She reached up and scratched in annoyance at a bug bite on the back of her shoulder, shaking the line again in an effort to catch the attention of a fish, any fish.

Yup, it sure was nice to have nothing to do but sit and gaze into space while waiting for the fish to bite.

Another peal of laughter drifted over and Jessie clenched her jaw. She held off for about four seconds and then her eyes flicked down to focus on Nick and Cindi again. Just what was so funny about fishing?

Jessie sighed. She had to get this stupid jealousy under control. Cindi made *her* laugh sometimes and you didn't see everyone else getting all bent out of shape about it.

What was Jessie so worried about anyway? It wasn't like they could do anything on camera.

She shifted on the rock, rubbing her thigh to ease out a cramp. She didn't care about winning the challenge at this stage. She just wished someone would catch something so she could give up on this lost cause. She scratched at her shoulder again and then froze, holding her breath. Had she imagined it? She held the rod steady, narrowing her eyes to try and see into the water. The sun was making shadows and reflections on the translucent surface, playing tricks with her eyes. She gasped as she felt another quick tug on the rod. The line tautened briefly, then went loose again.

"Here, fishy fish," she whispered. "There's a good fish." She had emptied her bag onto the rock and now, using it as a glove, she started to pull the line in gently, winding it around the fishing rod. She was hardly daring to breathe as she felt the resistance on the line.

Praying that it wouldn't turn out to be an old boot she continued to reel in the line, exactly as she'd seen Nick do on television.

She let out a yelp of excitement as the cod's tail flipped at the surface of the water and then she hoisted him out, yanking up the rod and line at the same time. She wound up the last of the line and held up her prize in triumph.

"Hey, guys!" she yelled out in delight. "Nick! Look, I caught one!"

They looked up and Nick started waving at her. Her heart swelled with pride as she waved the line with the flailing fish dangling on the end of it.

Nick's waving grew more frantic and his voice drifted up to her.

"Jessie! Look out!"

"Is everything on this island a mutant?" grumbled Jessie again.

She still couldn't believe she'd been attacked by a flock of seagulls. They had descended on her in a whirling mass of squawking and flapping, more like a marauding band of pterodactyls than normal birds as they savaged her hard-won prize.

Nick added a stock cube to the crab stew and smiled.

Jessie picked up the shell of the crab that he'd trapped and admired the fiery sheen of red and blue color.

"What are these called again?" she asked.

"Coconut crabs."

"I mean, just look at the sheer size of it," she said with a mixture of awe and horror. "One of these could practically take your hand off." She looked anxiously at Nick. "Please tell me that these monsters don't like human warmth and companionship at night."

Nick's smile broke through again as he shook his head. "You know, we're actually quite lucky here. We're missing three species that make life so uncomfortable in other parts of the world. No mosquitoes, no rats and no cockroaches. This is as close as you'll get to paradise."

Jessie smiled wryly. "I know. And I do appreciate it. It just takes some getting used to."

She looked up and made a point of smiling affably as Cindi walked back from her stint in the confession cam. Jessie was going to be nicer and stop blaming Cindi just because Nick found her attractive. At least Cindi had put her clothes back on.

Or maybe she'd just spoken too soon. Cindi sat down next to Malcolm and unbuttoned the top of her uniform. She slid it off her shoulders, turning her back towards Malcolm.

"Did I get burnt today?" she asked.

"Doesn't look like it," said Malcolm. "Not too much." He looked away hurriedly as she turned back, peering down and patting her fingers lightly on the swell of her breasts. "My skin feels a bit warm," she said.

Malcolm poked at the fire, his face reddening into an instant case of sunburn.

"I'm going to let this stew simmer for a while," said Nick. "Malcolm, you and Cindi can clean the fish. I'm going to get Jessie started on her shelter."

He rose smoothly to his feet and put out his hand, helping Jessie up. "C'mon," he said. "Let's put you to work."

Jessie smiled, telling herself it was because she was looking forward to building a shelter and not because Cindi's face was sullen as she did up her buttons.

JESSIE KNEW THAT WHEN NICK touched her it was purely platonic but that didn't mean it didn't affect her. She had watched him working with other people on television; sometimes teaching others his techniques, sometimes learning about particular customs from nomadic tribesmen or outback survivors. She'd seen him fall into easy cooperation and knew that when his shoulder bumped against hers or when he moved her hand to reposition it on an intersection of supporting branches it was with a completely casual detachment.

Like just now when he'd put his hand on her waist to push her gently to one side so that he could crouch beside her and interweave the branches through the sticks that she was holding. Jessie was staring hard at the sticks and her eyes were aching with the effort of not looking down at him. His shoulder nudged her knee as he worked and she glanced down to see his head only inches from her bare thigh. She bit her lip and looked up again, willing herself not to start trembling.

It didn't help that she'd finally put her finger on something that had been bothering her. She felt like a half-naked bimbo in this dress and there was no way she would have worn it of her own free will, but now that she *was* wearing it she couldn't help thinking that it should have resulted in a more obvious reaction from Nick.

She'd been testing her theory for the past fifteen minutes and so far, no matter how suddenly she turned around or how far she leaned over, she hadn't once caught Nick ogling either her front or back view.

She had caught Malcolm sneaking peeks and hadn't let on, not wanting to embarrass him, but it proved that the dress was working and, all modesty aside, she couldn't understand why Nick's eyes weren't out on stalks.

She realized unhappily that it only confirmed her imagined perception of him as a man of too much character to be distracted by something as blatant as a skimpy dress. Integrity and courage, those were the things that won the eye of a man like Nick. After all, despite his nomadic lifestyle, he was also in show business. Pneumatic overly made-up women were probably ten-a-penny to him.

Jessie had a momentary impulse to blurt out that hers were real but wisdom prevailed and she quashed it.

Anyway, it was probably just as well that Nick wasn't responding to her looks. After all, in spite of the occasional irresistible fantasy, she wasn't here to win Nick's eye, or any other part of him. It wouldn't really be fair to Tom.

She frowned. It was the first time she'd thought about Tom since she'd arrived on the island. She'd obviously blotted him from her mind, not surprising after what he'd said at the airport. She shook her head as if to clear it. That was one of her promises to herself, that as long as she was here she wouldn't have to think about Tom.

"You getting tired?" asked Nick, rising slowly from his crouch. He stretched his hands over hers to hold the branches. "I think you can let go," he said. "The leaves I've woven through should hold them."

Jessie smiled to herself as she took her hands away and ducked out under his arm. Her head only came up to his chin and it was a new experience to her to be the small one. Nick removed his hands slowly and they both stepped back to admire their handiwork.

The bed frame was made out of four logs and it was filled with moss, undergrowth and leaves as bedding. Nick had notched five strong branches together to form the framework for a triangular roof. They weren't expecting rain but Nick had pointed out that they were in the Tropics and the possibility couldn't be ruled out. He'd notched more branches into this framework and they'd woven in large leaves to make a thick, waterproof thatch.

Nick pointed out the main feature which differentiated her bed from his.

"See the way the sleeping platform is raised off the ground?" he said. "It's like a bunk bed. That way, lizards will simply scuttle under it, rather than being inclined to investigate."

Jessie gave him a heartfelt smile. "I appreciate that."

Their eyes met and she felt a sudden burst of warmth, low in her stomach.

"C'mon," he said cheerfully. "I think we've earned our dinner."

Jessie followed him, telling herself crossly to stop imagining things.

MALCOLM COULDN'T SEEM TO get over the fact that he'd caught the fish.

"It's lovely," Cindi answered as he asked her yet again how it was. "It's delicious and fantastic. It is, without a doubt, the best thing I've ever eaten in my whole life. Thank you so much for catching it, Malcolm, I will be in your debt forever."

Jessie couldn't help smiling. Okay, so Cindi was being a bit heavy on the sarcasm but Jessie had been about three seconds away from saying the same thing herself. To hear Malcolm going on you'd have thought he was working his way towards a doctorate in ichthyology.

"I'm just amazed that I actually caught three," Malcolm went on, undaunted. "Just with the rod standing in the sand. I wasn't even trying."

"Don't forget that I caught one, too," said Jessie. "I mean, if I could catch one they must have been throwing themselves out of the water."

"You're right," admitted Malcolm. "But if I'd built the raft and been able to get out to sea just imagine how many more I could have caught."

"Enough already!" exclaimed Cindi. "Could you stop rubbing it in? I was barely able to cast out a line. I mean, sheesh, you guys made hooks and everything. It's sickening."

"You shouldn't feel bad," said Malcolm. Jessie smiled at him. She liked the way he always rushed to make someone feel better.

"After all," he said, "I have got an unfair advantage, you know, because I'm a man."

He took another bite of his fish, oblivious to the electric silence.

Nick burst out laughing. "Oh, boy," he said, coughing as a bit of crab stew went down the wrong way. "Even on a bet, I wouldn't have said that."

Jessie and Cindi looked at each other and then back at Malcolm.

"I'll arm wrestle you right now if you like," said Jessie pleasantly. She lifted an arm and flexed it, showing off some extremely toned musculature.

Nick whistled, long and low. "You're in so much trouble, Malcolm."

Great, thought Jessie, now he thinks I'm an ox. Way to impress him.

"Two hours a day in the gym," piped up Cindi. "I'll be happy to take you on as well."

Malcolm looked from one woman to the other, unable to tell if they were joking or not. "That's okay," he said nervously.

"What's the matter?" said Jessie, batting her eyelashes like a Southern belle. "Afraid you'll have an unfair advantage, what with you being a man?"

Malcolm looked to Nick for help.

Nick shrugged. "You walked into it on your own."

"Okay," said Malcolm, throwing up his hands. "I'm sorry. I don't go to the gym and I have the muscles of a ten-year-old girl."

Jessie coughed.

"A ten-year-old boy!" Malcolm amended quickly. He sighed. "You two may as well just arm wrestle each other."

"See, that's just another of the many advantages of being female," explained Cindi as she accepted another plate of roasted fish and papaya from Nick. "We don't have to compete to prove ourselves."

Jessie smiled her agreement, feeling horribly deceitful inside. Cindi was so fun and guileless, and Jessie was definitely in competition with her.

As THEY FINISHED OFF the food Jessie reached up to scratch surreptitiously at the back of her head. A slight color rose in her cheeks as she caught Nick watching her.

"Are you sure there are no mosquitoes on this island?" she asked. "It feels like something's definitely been nibbling on me."

"It's the sand," Nick told her. "You need a wash in fresh water."

He picked up a stick and began to draw on a patch of

smooth sand. They all watched as a map of the island took shape.

"This is our camp," Nick pointed out. "There's the tiki hut and that's the promontory that Jessie was fishing from." He looked up and they exchanged a wry glance before he went on. "The island is about five miles by ten. There's a fresh water lagoon here, in the center of the east side. You go through the forest and there's a fairly gentle upward gradient all the way inland until you come to a steep rock face. It's about ten feet, but it's covered in vines and easy enough to climb. The lagoon is just above that. There's a waterfall and everything, it's beautiful." He kept sketching. "There's more forestation to the west, that's where I found the potatoes. There's also another beach diagonally across on the northwest corner."

A thought struck Jessie. "I've been meaning to ask, do you know exactly where the Island Eyes are?"

Nick shook his head. "Nope."

She shot him a teasing look. "I bet you do. Come on, Nick, you can tell us."

"I really don't. Anyway, you'll only make yourself crazy if you think too much about them. Even if you avoid one camera there'll be another one focused on you from another angle. Trust me, it'll be easier for you in the long run to just forget about them."

"Easy for you to say," remarked Cindi. "You're not trying to win a million bucks. You don't have to look good on camera."

"So that's the only reason you're here?" said Nick. "For the money?"

"Oh, no," said Cindi. "I'm mostly here for the experience. I'm really interested in learning about nature and, you know, living off the land and in harmony with it."

Jessie saw Malcolm trying to hide his smile and knew that his face was a mirror image of her own.

"Really?" said Nick innocently. "That's interesting. But didn't you say you were an actress?"

Cindi fidgeted, tracing her toe in the sand. "Yeah. So?"

"So you're here because you want to learn how to live off the land and it's got nothing to do with any exposure or publicity this might garner you?"

Cindi seemed to accept that it was a lost cause. "Okay, I admit it. But you can't blame me. I've been trying for years. You have no idea how hard it is to catch a break in this business." She shrugged. "And heck, I'll take the money, too, if it's going."

"I think Malcolm's already called dibs on that, hasn't he?" Jessie joked.

Nick turned to him with interest. "You're only here for the money?"

"I'm like Cindi," answered Malcolm. "I'll take it if it's going. But I really want the experience, too. I figure it's my last chance before..."

They all looked at him as he trailed off. He looked sheepishly at the fire and Jessie was struck by a horrible thought.

As was Cindi. "Oh, my God," she exclaimed. "You're dying!"

Malcolm looked up. "What?"

"This is your last chance to have some fun before you die," prompted Cindi. "That's why you're here, isn't it?"

Jessie gave her a look, trying to tell her to have some tact.

Malcolm looked aghast. "No! What are you talking about? I'm not dying."

Jessie turned to him. "You're not?" she blurted.

"No," he said again. "Of course not. I just meant that with Debbie and I expecting our first, life is going to be different from now on. I'll be a family man, with responsibilities. This is my last chance to be a..." he shook his head in embarrassment and mumbled "...a hero."

They all nodded in understanding, but smiles crept onto their faces.

"Jessie," said Nick hurriedly. "Why are you here?"

"Uh..." Jessie faltered, thinking fast. "I'm here for the money, of course. You know, a million bucks, phew, who wouldn't want that?"

"So you're not an aspiring actress or secretly expecting twins?" Nick teased.

"Neither," said Jessie firmly.

"What do you do?" asked Cindi.

"I'm a librarian."

Cindi looked aghast. "Oh, no," she said, covering her mouth. "I'm so sorry. I shouldn't have teased you about having sex with Nick."

Again, Jessie had the urge to put a big piece of duct tape over Cindi's mouth. She squinted at her.

"I said I'm a librarian," she clarified. "Not a *virgin*."

There was a long silence.

Jessie put her face in her hands. "I really wish I hadn't said that," she mumbled.

Cindi sighed in frustration. "*That's* what I should have said I was. A virgin who's only got a few weeks to live. Talk about audience pay dirt."

4

ALTHOUGH HER SLEEP had been fitful and disturbed—she'd woken up quite a few times disoriented by the leaves and the exotic perfume of the night air before remembering where she was—Jessie awoke in the morning feeling refreshed and enthusiastic for the day ahead.

She'd also stopped checking her bare wrist to find out what time it was. Time didn't matter here—they lived by daylight, or the lack of it. Relieved to find that she hadn't acquired any saurian sleeping partners during the night, Jessie stretched and yawned. She rubbed her face and clambered out of the shelter, waving amiably at Kenny who was sitting by the remains of last night's fire, camera trained patiently on her shelter.

"Morning all," said Jessie cheerfully to the camera lens. Kenny pointed towards her feet and Jessie looked down to see a package that was resting against her shelter. The wrapping was a thin, flexible piece of bark, wound into a tube and bound with strips of vine. Jessie smiled and sat down to unwrap it with a mounting curiosity. Her smile turned into a full-blown laugh when she took out a pair of shoes which were tightly woven out of strips of large leaves.

She held them up proudly for the camera and slipped one on. The leaves were a little coarse and scratchy but they were a perfect fit. She took a few experimental steps and was surprised to find that they held their shape and the layers of tough leaf provided a very good protection from the ground.

"Where's Nick?" she asked Kenny. He didn't answer, just pointed at the piece of bark that had been wrapped around her shoes. She picked it up and read the words scratched on the inside.

First to find me wins.

Jessie grinned and then looked over at the other shelters. She couldn't tell if there was anyone in them or not. She turned back to the camera and raised her eyebrows inquisitively. Kenny eventually relented and ducked his head out from behind the camera.

"Malcolm's gone," he said quietly. "Another cameraman's gone with him. I'm to follow you and Cindi isn't up yet."

"Which way did Nick go?" Jessie tried.

Kenny gave her a "yeah, right" look and tucked his head behind the eyepiece again. She went over to the fireside and took a drink of water and ate some leftover papaya. She grimaced as she reached up to scratch the nape of her neck. The sand in her scalp was really getting to her. She stretched, loosening her shoulders and decided to leave Nick's T-shirt on for a while. As she'd been going to bed the night before he'd handed it to her, without ceremony, and she'd taken it, equally casually. No one needed to know that, in bed, she'd pulled it briefly up to her nose and breathed in the scent of him before she'd let sleep take her.

Her glance fell on the patch of sand that Nick had been drawing on the night before and she looked at it thoughtfully. It was half kicked-over but Jessie remembered the way Nick had drawn it, the word lagoon crossing his lips more than once. She pondered for a moment then decided to follow her instinct, seeing as she hadn't any other ideas.

She looked down at her new moccasins and then up at the edge of the forest. Well, it was as good a place to start as any.

She decided that she could go a little way into the forest and if she felt like she was getting lost she could always backtrack.

WELL, YES, IN THEORY. The reality was that after ten minutes the undergrowth had swallowed up the path behind her and soon she was no longer sure if she was still heading inland or if she was just walking in a circle. There were twigs in her hair and a sheen of perspiration on her forehead. She fluttered her hand, fighting off yet another strange bug as it made a kamikaze dive for her face, and she searched the undergrowth for the elusive incline that Nick had described.

She looked back to see Kenny stumbling courageously after her. Unlike her, he didn't have the luxury of being able to look down at where he was going so his progress was more perilous and halting. On the other hand, at least his amateurish meanderings weren't being recorded for posterity.

"Okay," said Jessie, trying to show a lot more hope and enthusiasm than she was actually feeling. "We'll go in this direction for another ten minutes and then, if that doesn't pan out we'll...umm..."

"We'll what?" said Kenny with a trace of weariness.

Jessie pretended not to hear him. She was wondering about that herself.

"THIS IS IT," said Jessie. "I'm sure of it." It had been almost ninety minutes since they'd started out and Kenny had broken down and eaten his lunch, a ham baguette with all the trimmings. It had taken every ounce of Jessie's willpower to resist the urge to cheat, especially when Kenny had been willing to share and it would have been so easy.

Jessie's stomach growled in yet another rebuke of her morality and she focused hard on the towering cliff face ahead of them.

"He described it as a bit of a stiff climb but not impossible. This must be it."

Kenny shook his head. "There's no way I'll get up there with all this gear. I'll have to wait for you here." He didn't sound too upset about it.

Jessie turned to look at the vine-covered cliff face again, her spirits rising at the thought that she might actually have reached her destination.

She rubbed her hands together briskly before putting her foot into the first craggy foothold and reaching for a vine to pull herself up. She soon found that it did in fact look more forbidding and difficult than it actually was. There were many deep footholds in the rock and the vines were a strong support. She reached the top and pulled herself over the lip of the cliff, her face flushed with triumph. There were more trees and undergrowth but Jessie pushed through them with determination until she suddenly found herself on the edge of an utterly breathtaking vista.

The lagoon was a deep, crystalline blue, surrounded on three sides by the forest. Across from Jessie a two-tiered waterfall cascaded down the cliff-face, the water glinting and sparkling as it tumbled over the moss-dappled rock. The air was rich with the perfume of the hibiscus plants that bordered the lagoon, their flowers a blaze of bright reds, oranges and yellows. There was the low hum of insects and the occasional squawk from deep in the forest.

As Jessie watched, mesmerized by the idyllic scene, there was a splash and Nick's dark hair suddenly broke through the surface of the water. He shook his head and drops sprayed off in a glittering corona.

He didn't notice Jessie as he dived under again, a dark shadow moving through the water before resurfacing on the other side of the lagoon with the same exuberant shake of his head.

Jessie laughed and called out to him. "Am I first?"

He looked over. "We have a winner!"

Jessie raised her hands in excited triumph. "I couldn't have done it without the shoes," she said generously.

He laughed, treading water. "Congratulations." He looked around. "Wasn't Kenny supposed to be with you?"

Jessie pointed behind her. "Kenny's at the bottom of the cliff. I'm afraid we took quite a circuitous route to get here and the cliff face was the final straw for him. I think he's going to wait for you to bring us back."

Nick laughed again. "Well, you look like you could use a swim. Are you coming in?"

Jessie suddenly became conscious of her appearance. She realized she must look pretty flushed and sweaty and a swim was about as close to heaven as she could imagine. She walked over to the edge of the lagoon and bent down to dip her fingers in the water. It even *felt* clean.

She stood up again and pulled off the T-shirt, dropping it on top of Nick's other clothes. She glanced at him again as she began to take off her shoes. She blinked and looked away hurriedly then snuck another peek to confirm what she'd seen.

Oh, boy, she thought, looking away again. Even though the water blurred the details she'd seen enough to realize that Nick was completely naked.

She took her time removing her shoes, making a job out of it while she tried to decide what to do.

She'd initially thought that she'd just take her shoes off and jump in with her dress on. But now that the thought of skinny-dipping had entered her mind she was surprised to find herself actually considering it. It would be so glorious to slide into that warm water, to feel it flowing over her skin. To drift and float like a true island babe, getting back to nature.

Yeah right. Like it was really going to happen. Like she'd

really peel off her dress in front of Nick. Flimsy as it was, it did at least keep her decent.

Even as her thoughts occasionally strayed into indecency.

Anyway, even if Nick hadn't been there, there were still the Island Eyes to consider. Maybe Nick could be fairly confident that no naked footage of him would reach the small screen but Jessie wasn't about to chance it.

Anyway, she couldn't sit here all day, pretending to take her shoes off. Time for a swim.

She stood up and stretched her arms out, tantalizing herself with another moment's delay. She glanced at Nick and was about to lower herself into the water when she spotted movement at the base of the waterfall. She hesitated.

Sunlight flashed off the water, blinding her and she put up her hand to shade her eyes, peering at the churning water under the waterfall. Was there something there?

She squinted and saw the shape again. Long and dark, it drifted out from beneath the falling water, barely breaking the surface.

Jessie looked at Nick. It seemed to be heading in his direction. She looked back at the shape again and suddenly recognized the long, scaly back for what it was.

She gave a sharp intake of breath. What on earth was Lois thinking? She knew the producer was hungry for ratings but this was ridiculously dangerous.

"Nick. Psst, Nick," said Jessie, struggling to keep her voice calm.

"Yup?" he said, treading water lazily, his eyes closed against the sun.

"Nick, I want you to get out of the water. Right now."

Nick's eyes opened. "What?"

Jessie beckoned. "Swim towards me, as quietly as you can. Now, Nick. I mean it."

Frowning in bemusement, Nick started a lazy crawl towards her, his strong body propelling him effortlessly through the water.

Jessie's eyes darted back and forth between Nick and the threat that he was so blithely oblivious to, even as it continued to glide steadily towards him. When he reached the edge she gestured again.

"Come on, get out."

Nick looked up at her. "I don't know if you realize this but I'm kind of naked here."

"I know, but this is no time for shyness, believe me. Just do as I say."

Nick shrugged. "Okay, lady, you're the boss."

Putting his hands on the edge he hoisted himself out of the water. Jessie's heart skipped as all six foot three inches of tanned glory emerged, wet muscles glistening. She couldn't help having one look—although she resolutely kept her eyes above the waistline—and then she had to force herself to tear her eyes away.

She let out a breath she didn't even know she'd been holding.

"I'm sorry about the drama," she said. "But I didn't want to make you panic." She held out a trembling finger. "I'm afraid that Lois got her alligator after all."

Nick followed the line of her finger. Jessie looked up at him as his brow furrowed and a muscle twitched in his jaw. He looked down at her and she could see a light shining in his eyes.

"I don't believe it," he breathed. "You saved my life."

Jessie lowered her eyes bashfully then hurriedly raised them again.

"If only there was something I could do," Nick continued. "Some way to show my gratitude."

Jessie bit her lip. "It's okay," she said. "I didn't really do anything except act on instinct."

"Even so," Nick said with fervor. "I owe you my life. Another few moments and who knows what might have happened?"

Jessie was beginning to feel a little self-conscious. "I'm sure you would have spotted him yourself sooner or later."

"There's only one thing to do," said Nick, lifting his chin and narrowing his eyes. "I have to make this island safe for you. I'm going to wrestle him. With my bare hands!"

With this announcement, Nick dived headfirst into the lagoon.

"No, Nick, what are you doing?" Jessie clamped her hands over her eyes, then separated her fingers so she could peer through them in horror. "Please come back."

Nick ignored her as he sped towards the alligator. Jessie moaned in distress as they met in the middle of the lagoon with a huge splash. Water churned and Jessie caught one last glimpse of legs and arms flailing before she covered her eyes completely.

When she heard laughter she decided she must be having an auditory hallucination.

Because alligators didn't laugh...right?

She moved her pinkie finger and peeked out. She slowly removed her hands from her face and frowned in bewilderment. Nick was cheerfully swimming back towards her, pushing a log sideways in front of him. Jessie's eyes darted around for the deadly predator before coming to rest on Nick's gleeful expression.

Once again, Jessie brought her hands up to cover her face.

"Another mighty foe crushed in the hands of Nick Garrett," she heard him say as he reached the edge of the lagoon.

"I don't believe this," mumbled Jessie.

Nick didn't reply and she eventually took down her hands and met his eyes. He had his arms folded and resting on the bank and he was looking up at her, a huge grin on his face.

As mortified as she was, she couldn't help smiling. "It really looked like an alligator from far away."

"I'm sure it did," said Nick. "And you know what? I do appreciate you saving my life even though I wasn't actually in any danger."

Jessie nodded meekly, admitting that yes, mistakes like that were easy to make after all.

"It's always better to be safe than sorry," continued Nick with an air of satisfaction.

"All right," said Jessie. "I get it, okay?" Her hand flew to her mouth as another thought struck her. "Oh, no!"

Nick widened his eyes theatrically. "What is it? A lion? A gorilla? A dinosaur?"

His impudence made it a lot easier for Jessie to tell him. "None of the above. I just realized that you were naked on camera."

His smile didn't waver. "No, I wasn't."

"Sorry to have to contradict you," said Jessie, not the slightest bit sorry, "but you were."

Nick pushed back from the edge and turned over lazily, drifting away from her. "There are no cameras up here," he called over his shoulder. He stopped and turned again, kicking languidly. "Coming in?"

His look was innocent, but Jessie thought she felt an unspoken communication flash between them. Unfortunately she didn't know him well enough to decipher it.

Was he telling her that there was no one watching so she should feel free to skinny-dip if she wanted to?

Or was it a more overt invitation? Join me in this naked paradise and let's see where it leads to?

Or would he simply be surprised, and maybe alarmed, if she did suddenly start stripping? Would he hop out of the water and start putting on his clothes in a hurry?

Well, it didn't really matter what he was saying. Cameras or no cameras Jessie was still a long way from baring her all.

Pausing just long enough to remove her microphone, she sat on the edge of the lagoon and slid into the water. Her dress needed a wash anyway.

Her skin tingled in the warm water and within seconds she was imitating a seal herself, laughing and diving and splashing with abandon. She drifted out to the middle of the lagoon, moving her arms and legs lazily as she floated on her back.

"This is heaven," she called to Nick, who was swimming some feet away.

He gave her a smile, eyes glinting and Jessie felt her chest constrict.

It can't possibly be heaven, she thought, not with such a wicked temptation right in front of me. What would he do, she wondered, if I swam over and wrapped my long legs around his thighs? Would he be inclined to wrestle *me* with his bare hands?

"How do you know there are no cameras here?" she asked, wrestling her thoughts back into line.

"Spencer, one of the technical guys, told me. He's overseeing most of the visuals so he told me they'd left this whole area uncovered."

Nick paused in his swimming and spoke thoughtfully. "Unless of course there's another lagoon exactly like this somewhere else on the island."

Jessie laughed. "Too late now."

They drifted in silence for another few moments, Jessie trying desperately to think of anything except his golden, toned body, mere meters away from hers.

She swam over to the waterfall and found that there was a low shelf rock under the surface of the water. She stood up on it and, with her eyes closed, let the falling water wash over her, rinsing the sand and salt from her hair and skin. She couldn't help wondering if Nick wanted something to happen. The lack of cameras, his nakedness, it was almost as if he'd set up the opportunity. And if so, would it have made any difference to him if Cindi had come along first?

But she hadn't. Jessie had found him. The question was, now, was she going to do anything about it?

She stepped out from under the waterfall and wiped the water from her face, taking a deep breath as she opened her eyes.

Nick, fully dressed again, waved to her from the opposite bank.

Jessie's shoulders slumped. Yeah, she said to herself, like you really would have done it. She slid back into the water and swam over to him, pulling herself up onto the bank and dropping onto the grass.

"Feeling better?" said Nick.

"About a million times better," she said, squeezing the water out of her hair and shaking it out to dry. She lifted her face to the warmth of the sun, then squealed as a long-legged bug flew drunkenly past her face.

"Every time I relax they come out of nowhere to get me," she sighed.

Nick laughed, plucking at blades of grass. "Didn't you ever go camping as a kid?" he asked. "Or are you a born and bred city girl?"

Jessie smiled. "I don't think Fairbury could be described as a city. It's stretching it a bit to call it a town. Sure, I went camping a few times as a kid on school outings. But, somehow, when a hundred kids descend on a place, nature doesn't get that much of a look-in. You could hardly call it a survival situation."

"Fairbury?" asked Nick. "Where is that?"

"Iowa," said Jessie. "State flower, the wild rose. State bird, the eastern goldfinch. Area, 56, 276 square miles."

"Oh, that's right," smiled Nick. "I would expect the local librarian to know all that."

Jessie was pleased that he'd remembered, though she wasn't sure if his comment was a compliment or not.

"So you've lived there all your life?" he asked.

She nodded. "Anyway, what about you? Would I be right in guessing that you were raised by wolves?"

Nick laughed. "My dad worked as a forest ranger in the Absaroka Range in Yellowstone National Park and he took myself and my brothers with him every chance he got. Two of my brothers became rangers and the other is in Africa, working with a conservation group. I spent a lot of years with them myself."

"And how do you make the step from that to television?" asked Jessie, genuinely curious.

"There was a TV crew from Quest Broadcasting making a series of programs on disappearing species and I went out with them to help them get footage of sable antelopes and then they asked if I'd help on some other projects. I did consulting work for a few years and on one of those jobs I met Lois. She was the one who first suggested I host my own show."

"Was it something you'd already thought about doing?"

Nick wrinkled his nose. "Not really. I thought at first that Lois wanted me to make a macho man show with lots of emphasis on overpowering nature and dominating wildlife but after a few meetings I realized she was interested in filming me doing all the things I'd normally be doing anyway and, at the risk of sounding preachy, that it would be a forum to educate people about the natural world."

Jessie smiled with affection. A less apposite word to describe Nick couldn't be found. It was precisely his lack of preachiness that had made *Survive This!* such a runaway success.

On camera Nick made no secret of his feelings, whether it was trepidation at dealing with poisonous spiders or unbridled amusement at the sight of cavorting lion cubs. He was equally unpretentious when describing the properties of exotic plants or breathlessly relating the dangers of unpredictable weather systems.

Jessie suddenly realized that she was gazing fondly at him again and she quickly tilted her head back up to the sun, trying to think of another question to break the silence.

"What's been your worst experience?" she asked at last. "Any really hair-raising near-death moments?"

Nick flicked an ant from his knee. "It isn't actually the near-death experiences that are the worst," he said thoughtfully. "When you get bitten by a snake or fall overboard or come face-to-face with a bear there's just so much adrenaline pumping through you that there's no time to do anything but react. By the time you get around to being scared it's all over, one way or another." He lay back, resting his weight on his elbows. "What I really find hard to handle is consistently extreme conditions. When it's very, very hot or very, very cold and there's no change in sight. Humidity's a killer, too. I think that unrelenting discomfort is more wearing than a quick burst of terror. Hey, look at that."

He was pointing up towards the trees at the top of the waterfall. Jessie squinted. "What?"

He edged over to her and put his arm up, giving her a sightline. A jolt of electricity pulsed through Jessie at the touch of his arm against her shoulder but she ignored it. She was working on the theory that if she steadfastly ignored these sparks they would eventually go away. Then she let out a gasp as she spotted two parrotlike birds with the most beautiful vibrant plumage she had ever seen. They were like live opals in the foliage. Nick lay back on the grass, looking completely relaxed, and Jessie tried to remember what they'd been talking about.

"If you're not going to describe your worst experience," she teased, "you have to at least show me your best scar."

Nick laughed. "Let's see," he said. "My *best* scar. That would have to be this one." He pulled up his trouser leg and held out his calf for inspection.

Jessie's eyes widened as she took in the long, white scar that snaked all the way from his ankle to the back of his knee.

"White-water rafting," Nick explained. "On the Flathead River, in Montana. I got tossed from my kayak and torn up on the rocks."

Jessie shook her head as she listened, awed and amazed.

"Oh," he added with boyish enthusiasm. "I guess this one is pretty glamorous." He lifted up his T-shirt and turned sideways to show her three parallel marks running along his waist.

"Leopard," he said. "In Angola. We'd tranquillized him but I went in too soon and he took a swipe at me. I was pretty lucky. A little deeper and he'd have removed a kidney for me."

After Jessie had taken a long look, complete with admiring grimace, Nick pulled down his T-shirt again and gave her a grin.

"Go on," he said. "It's your turn."

Jessie shook her head. "I don't have any scars."

"Everyone has scars."

Jessie was about to deny it again but then she nodded and held up her hand to reveal a tiny white mark at the knuckle of her thumb.

"This is one that I'm especially proud of," she said. "It happened to me while I was slicing a bagel."

"Don't tell me…"

"Yes," she concurred. "I had my thumb through the hole in the middle."

Nick winced.

"You don't do that twice," she said with a smile.

"No kidding."

"And here's another," said Jessie, remembering. "Actually, I don't know if it's still there, I haven't looked at it for a while." She pulled her hair back from her forehead and leaned forward so Nick could examine her hairline.

"Yeah, I can see it. Scalp wound." He nodded knowledgably. "There must have been a lot of blood."

"There was," said Jessie. "Gary Patton threw a snowball with a stone in the middle of it. The little jerk, he nearly knocked me unconscious."

Nick made a sympathetic face. "Did you get him back?"

Jessie gave him a mock sorrowful look. "Well, it was decided that such a dangerous creature couldn't be allowed to roam free and he had to be put down."

Nick imitated her gravity. "That happens. Nature can be cruel."

Jessie giggled, her eyes growing distant as she reminisced. "Actually, Ralph Cassidy did try to beat him up on my behalf, but Gary really was a little thug and Ralph came off the worse for it." She sighed. "He was my first kiss."

"The little thug?" asked Nick in alarm.

Jessie laughed. "Ralph! My knight in shining armor. Well, heck, he deserved something for his troubles."

"Betty Myers was my first kiss," said Nick. "I dared her to eat worms and she did, so I kissed her."

Jessie wrinkled her nose in polite repulsion. "That's the worst first kiss story I've ever heard."

Nick looked sheepish. "It is, isn't it? I keep reminding myself to make up a new one. So, what happened with you and Ralph Cassidy? Was it true love for two weeks?"

"Two days I think. Then my height became a problem. He couldn't handle the fact that his girlfriend was two inches taller than him." She shrugged. "That was pretty much the story of my youth and adolescence." Her tone was light but Jessie still felt a little stab of hurt when she remembered the awkwardness of being the tallest person in the class.

"I was a bit of a misfit, too," said Nick. "Always messing around with some science project, more comfortable in the company of animals than humans."

He grinned at her and for the first time Jessie felt that maybe it wasn't too bad to have been an odd one out.

She closed her eyes, raising her face to the sun again and sighed with pleasure. The air was warm and sweet with the fragrance of hibiscus and the grass was soft under her bare thighs.

She opened her eyes lazily and tilted her head to look at Nick again. He was watching her and he didn't look away as their eyes met. Jessie held his gaze, marveling at the color of his eyes close-up, a greenish blue that seemed to reflect light like one of the beach rock pools.

"Hello!" came Kenny's voice, a rude interruption in the stillness of the moment. "Can you hear me? Are you guys up there?"

"OH, GOOD," SAID CINDI, emerging stiffly from her shelter. "I thought I'd slept in. Boy, I was really tired."

Jessie and Nick grinned at each other as Cindi rubbed her eyes and then picked up the piece of bark that was lying in front of her shelter.

"First to find me wins," she read out. She looked up at Nick. "Wow," she said dryly. "That's quite a challenge."

Jessie sat down and took off her moccasins. She dropped the selection of fruit that she and Nick had gathered on the way back and shook out her hair which had almost dried fully in the sun.

"So what do we have to do?" asked Cindi. "Close our eyes and count to a hundred?"

Nick set about rekindling the embers of last night's fire. "It's already done," he explained. "Jessie found me."

"He was at the lagoon," explained Jessie. "You should see it, it's so gorgeous."

Cindi's face dropped. "I can't believe it," she said in disappointment. "I *did* sleep in."

"Never mind," said Nick. "You probably needed it."

"Not as much as I needed to win a challenge point," Cindi grumbled.

"Is Malcolm back yet?" asked Jessie.

"What?" said Cindi. "He's gone, too? Why didn't any of you wake me?"

Jessie busied herself with storing the fruit, reminding herself that all was fair in love and war.

"Malcolm's not back yet?" said Nick, looking around. He jumped up from the fire and went to talk to Kenny who was changing the tape in his camera.

"Stoke up the fire and boil some water," he called over to Cindi and Jessie a few minutes later. "And then gather some more firewood. I think I'd better go see where Malcolm's got to."

JESSIE DROPPED ANOTHER armload of sticks onto the stack of firewood and she put her hands on her hips.

Cindi was standing on one leg, with one arm stretched out in front of her and the other holding up her other leg behind her. She was gazing upwards as she talked.

"...of course it took me some time to realize that he was a deadbeat but guess I was just more gullible when I was younger. Who isn't, right? But I figured I couldn't deny him his dreams when I had artistic ambitions of my own. And he had such a great voice. Just no discipline unfortunately."

Jessie frowned. Had Cindi even noticed she'd been gone? As she watched, Cindi came out of the pose and sat down, crossing her legs and putting her hands up in a prayerful position in front of her. Kenny circled her slowly.

"But things definitely work out for a reason because if we'd still been together when I made the commercial, that money would have been so gone. On a new guitar probably."

Jessie took the boiling water off the fire and replaced the pot with another one, putting the hot water aside to cool. She wiped the back of her hand across her perspiring face, noticing too late how dirty her hand was. Wonderful.

"And I was so upset when my scene got cut from that movie but I see now that that was for the best, too. I mean, I really thought that was going to be my big break but then I probably would have ended up working on some other movie and I wouldn't have been able to come on this show."

Cindi lifted her arms above her head, her bosom rising majestically. The pink underwear was on full display again. Jessie picked at some dirt under her fingernails, trying to gather the enthusiasm to go for more firewood.

"My parents weren't too happy, of course," Cindi droned on. "But they haven't been happy since I told them I wanted to be an actress in the first place. It's natural, I guess, because it's such a hard thing to break into but I guess I was hoping they'd understand that I have to try."

Jessie fiddled with a lock of hair, combing it out between her fingers. Funny, she'd always thought yoga was a silent activity.

"I guess I've showed them in the end. I bet your parents were always happy with you though, being a librarian?"

Jessie didn't look up. She picked some more dirt out from her fingernails.

"Jessie?"

Jessie waited another beat before giving in. "Yes?" she said absently.

"Your parents," prompted Cindi. "How did they take it when you told them about this?"

Jessie spoke calmly. "Oh, my parents are dead." She put on her standard serene face. "They died when I was quite young."

"Oh, my God," said Cindi. "That's a bummer."

Jessie's mask slipped a little. No one had ever described it quite like that before.

"I'll tell you something," Cindi said, straightening out her legs and stretching down over them. "There are times when I could have done without my parents on my back. I bet you got away with lots of stuff when you were a teenager."

Jessie felt a knot of irritation form in her chest. "It doesn't really work like that."

"Were you put in an orphanage or something?"

"I was raised by my grandparents," said Jessie.

"That's not so bad," said Cindi. "You were one of the lucky ones." She smiled at Jessie. "They obviously did a great job with you."

"Thanks," said Jessie, keeping a firm lid on her emotions. "I think I'll go and get some more wood."

"Sure," said Cindi. She got up and shook herself. "Oh, that feels good. Have you ever done yoga?"

"Nope," said Jessie, heading for the forest.

"You should," said Cindi fervently. "It's very good exercise."

Jessie paused and looked back, wondering if Cindi was being ironic.

It seemed not.

"I think I'll just stick to gathering firewood for now," said Jessie.

"So what happened with you and Nick?"

Jessie stopped again and turned, tilting her head warily. "What?"

"At the lagoon," said Cindi as she slipped into her chambermaid's uniform again. "Did you two get up to any hanky-panky?"

"What?" said Jessie. "No. Don't be ridiculous. Of course not." She looked at Kenny who had suddenly decided to start filming her. Not while she was tending the camp and gathering supplies, no, of course not, he had to film her while she was babbling and trying not to blush.

Cindi closed her eyes and rolled her head from side to side. Then she breathed in deeply and fixed her eyes on Jessie.

"Don't think I won't fight you for him," she said in a low, threatening tone.

Kenny's camera snapped around.

Jessie took a step back, surprised by the intensity of Cindi's stare. "What?"

"I love him," said Cindi. "I've always loved him. And if you think I'm letting him go to you or anyone else, well, you're making the biggest mistake of your life."

Jessie was frozen. She had never felt herself the focus of so much hatred, all the more frightening because it had come out of nowhere. She felt transfixed, as if by a viper.

"Cindi," she said in bemusement, "I don't know what you're talking about. I don't...I don't want him."

"Don't lie to me!" Jessie was dismayed to see Cindi's eyes filling with tears. She put up her hands in a placating gesture as Cindi let loose another torrent of angry words. "I've seen the way you look at him, the way you're throwing yourself at him. You're not the first, don't you understand? And sure, maybe you'll take him for a night or a week, but it's me he's coming home with." Cindi thumped her chest as her tears spilled over. "Me! You'll never have him because he belongs to me!"

Jessie's heart was hammering as adrenaline coursed through her. She couldn't believe that Lois had let such a crazed fanatic on the island with Nick. For now though, she had to worry about herself. She circled around the fire as Cindi lurched towards her.

"Cindi, please," she said as softly as she could. "Please calm down. I'm sure this is all a mistake that we can sort out."

Cindi swayed, an expression of infinite sadness clouding her face. She dropped to her knees and more tears rolled silently down her cheeks as she wrapped her arms around herself. "Don't you understand?" she said, plaintive as a child. "That I can't live without him? He's my world."

"Okay," said Jessie soothingly. "That's okay. You're all right." She looked up at Kenny who was still filming, albeit from a safe distance. *Get Nick!* she mouthed vehemently. She looked back at Cindi and her pulse went into overdrive again as Cindi stood up, brushing the tears from her face. Cindi smiled and Jessie took a cautious step back.

Cindi turned to Kenny. "Ta-daa!" she said, taking a bow. She turned back to Jessie. "What did you think? Be honest. Was it a bit much, the way I fell to my knees? Should I have kept the anger going a bit more?"

Jessie stared at her as she went on speculatively, gesticulating as she spoke. "I wanted to make a rapid transition though, you know, anger to grief."

Jessie sank onto the log by the fire, her breathing shallow. "I thought you were..."

"Mad?" suggested Cindi happily. She looked at the camera and spoke earnestly. "I could tone it down, if I had to."

Then she looked back at her unwitting co-star. "Hey, you were great, too."

Jessie looked up at her, still stunned.

"Sorry I couldn't warn you," said Cindi. "But I needed an authentic reaction, to make it believable. Hey, come on, admit it, it was kinda fun, wasn't it? Whaddya say we go get some firewood?"

THE FIRST THING THAT NICK noticed, as he and Malcolm walked back into the camp, was Jessie's face.

"Are you okay?" he asked. "You look a bit shaken."

She looked up from the fire in a distracted manner and her eyes darted to Cindi. A look passed between them and then a sparkle of amusement lit Jessie's eyes. The two women burst into laughter.

"I'm fine," said Jessie.

Nick decided not to press it, half afraid that it might be something to do with him.

"Well, are you all ready for your next challenge? I think you'll like it. Come with me."

"Are we going far?" said Cindi, getting panicked. "Should we bring anything?"

"You can if you want to," said Nick, striding off and leaving them no choice but to follow.

After a short trek through the forest they came to a clearing where Lois's crew had been busy the previous afternoon.

In the middle of the clearing was a large circular pit, measuring 100 feet in diameter. It was about ten feet deep and in the middle, pristine and incongruous, was a white box, half a meter square.

"The mystery prize is in that box," Nick told them. "First person to get it and bring it up out of the pit can have it and will also win the challenge point." He checked his watch. "You've got exactly one hour."

He strolled over and sat under a tree, stretching his arms up behind his head and watching them. This was going to be interesting.

The three stood on the edge of the pit, peering down. The sides were smooth and vertical and it was obviously too far to jump down.

Malcolm was the first to move. His checked his own watch and then he raced into the trees where he could be seen rooting frantically on the ground for fallen branches.

Cindi looked over at Nick. "It's impossible."

Nick didn't say anything. He smiled and shook his head.

Cindi frowned and looked back down at the pit. "I don't get it."

Nick shrugged. It wasn't impossible, but with the time limit he'd imposed there was only one solution. The fun part was seeing who'd work it out first.

Jessie was walking slowly around the circumference. She was nibbling on the edge of her thumb and her brow was furrowed. She stopped and sat down on the edge of the pit, her legs dangling over the side. She gazed alternately down at the ground far below and then up at the treetops, her eyes thoughtful and distant.

Then she glanced over as Cindi let out a yelp and pulled fishing line from the pocket of her uniform.

"I forgot I had this. I can use it right?" Cindi peered at Nick, daring him to forbid her.

He nodded. His eyes darted back to Jessie. She hadn't moved. She watched as Cindi tied the line onto a branch and attempted to hook the box.

Nick couldn't see down to the bottom of the pit from where he was sitting but he could tell from Cindi's face that her excitement had been premature and misplaced. Still, she kept trying doggedly, her tongue poking out of the corner of her mouth.

Jessie also watched as Malcolm brought back a bundle of sticks.

"Okay," he said maniacally. "Now I just need two long ones." Nick smiled to himself. Malcolm, still thinking linearly. Cindi, on the other hand, had stopped thinking altogether. She was tossing the line repeatedly at the box, letting out grunts and squeaks of annoyance.

Another five minutes ticked by.

Nick watched Jessie through half-closed eyes. He wondered what was going on in her head. He didn't think she'd given up. He smiled inwardly as he remembered her futile attempts to fight off the gulls the evening before. Then he caught his lip between his teeth as he remembered the way he'd behaved at the lagoon.

He wasn't quite sure what had gotten into him. With anyone else he would have just diplomatically pointed out that the predatory threat was in fact a piece of dead wood but for some reason he'd gone into a whole pantomime act for her.

As if he'd been showing off. It had taken him a while to identify it because he couldn't remember ever actually doing it before.

Well, sure, as a kid. Dad, Dad, look at me! Watch me jumping/diving/throwing/catching, etc. Kids showed off, that was natural. But it was disconcerting to find himself doing it at his age.

But it was the only way to describe it. He'd been showing off. Acting the fool to make her laugh.

He focused again as he saw her nod to herself. Once, then again. She looked up suddenly and caught his eyes, her face alive with satisfaction.

"Give up?" he teased.

"It's impossible," she said.

Cindi looked at her, then over at Nick in outrage.

Nick waited.

"For one person," said Jessie. She looked at Malcolm who was still rushing back and forth, trying to find two sticks that were long enough to reach the bottom of the pit. "You'll never make a ladder in time. We all have to work together."

Cindi's fishing rod had gone limp in her hand. "Is that right?" she asked Nick. He made a zipping motion across his lips.

Malcolm had stopped working. His face was red and creased with indecision and his breath was coming in short puffs.

"It's the only way," argued Jessie. "One person can be lowered down and they throw the stuff up from the box and then they stand on the box and the others pull them out."

"What if the prize is too heavy to throw?" Malcolm countered.

"Then two of us go down."

Cindi added her voice. "What if the box can't be moved? What if the prize can't be taken out of it?"

Jessie spread her hands. "Unknown variables," she admitted. "We can't do anything about them."

"But if we do it this way, who wins the challenge point?" Cindi added.

"We forfeit it," said Jessie. "At least this way we'll get the prize. We can share it."

"What if it's something that can't be shared?" Malcolm's face was a picture of distress.

Jessie shrugged. "It'll still be better than no one getting it."

They all exchanged glances, mulling it over.

"Thirty-five minutes left," Nick informed them.

"I don't know," said Malcolm, looking desperately between his ladder and the pit, trying to figure out some other way.

Jessie was still sitting calmly on the edge of the pit. Nick could see that her composure was due to the fact that she'd already made peace with her decision. As far as she was concerned, it was the only way. He quashed a smile of admiration, reminding himself that he wasn't supposed to have favorites.

"She's right," said Cindi suddenly, throwing her line aside. "Come on, Malcolm, you know she is. Let's just do it."

"Okay," said Malcolm. "We'll forfeit the point and if the prize is something that can't be divided we'll draw straws."

"Agreed," said Jessie. "Cindi, we'll lower you down, you're the lightest."

Cindi looked into the pit and then nodded in resignation. "Fine," she said. "But if it's food I'm staying down there and eating it all myself." She caught the look on Malcolm's face. "Joke!"

Malcolm and Jessie leaned over the edge and lowered Cindi down until she was about three feet from the bottom. She jumped down and hurried over to the box, opening it in excitement.

"Oh, you guys," her voice came up, echoing from the depths. "It's shower stuff! Gel, shampoo... Oh, wow, there's toothpaste!"

Malcolm and Jessie high-fived each other.

Five minutes later, and with ten minutes to spare on the deadline, Cindi and the precious cargo had been rescued.

Nick joined them as they cooed over their haul.

"Very good," he said. "I'm proud of you all. Within the time limit there wasn't any other way and, for being the first to say it, Jessie gets the point."

They all looked up. Jessie frowned, looking upset.

"No," she said. "We're forfeiting it."

Nick shook his head. "Nope, you don't get to do that. You can share the prize, but the point is yours."

Jessie smiled sheepishly at the others. "Sorry."

"Wait a minute," said Malcolm suspiciously. "You were the first one to find Nick this morning and then you're the one who knew what to do in this situation. Are you sure you haven't been getting any hints?"

5

LOIS TAPPED HER PEN on her clipboard.

"Well, kids," she announced. "We've got a real winner on our hands. Audience figures are climbing by the day and the feedback has been incredible. Our regular fan base hasn't been put off by the difference in format and we're tapping into a whole new demographic."

Jessie felt the uneasy fluttering in her rib cage that she always did when she heard about the people who were watching them. Maybe Nick was right and the less they thought about the outside world the better. Unfortunately, Lois wasn't allowing them that luxury. She was still raving about the viewing figures. Thousands of people. Hundreds of thousands. All watching and talking about it.

Many of whom probably suspected now that Jessie was cheating. Jessie was surprised to find that although most of her brain was horrified by this prospect there was also a part of it that was busy calculating whether or not that might gain her some audience support from people who admired that sort of ruthlessness.

Nick had leaped to her defense immediately the night before and between them they'd embarrassed Malcolm into recanting his accusation, but Jessie was under no illusions about what Lois, with her judicious use of editing, could do.

She tuned back into what Lois was saying.

"...and our polls are garnering an unprecedented response."

"Polls?" asked Jessie.

"That's right," said Lois. "On the Web site. Fun stuff, you know. We're telling people to log on and vote for things like who's going to win the next challenge, who'll be the last one up each morning, who's going to lose their temper first."

Jessie and the others made cringing faces at each other and laughed in self-conscious embarrassment.

Lois went on enthusiastically. "How many days before Cindi and Jessie end up in a catfight and what will it be about? Who's got the biggest skeleton in the closet and what is it? Will anyone sustain injuries? Which woman will get Nick? Will Malcolm cheat on his wife and with who? That sort of thing."

Everyone's eyes started to bug out.

Nick folded his arms and shook his head. "I just want you all to know that none of that was my idea."

Lois fired a look at him. "It's just a bit of fun," she scolded.

"I am not going to cheat on my wife," said Malcolm indignantly.

Jessie couldn't help looking at Cindi and she felt laughter threatening as they shared a look that said, *not with either one of us anyway, buddy.*

Lois flipped busily through the pages on her clipboard. "And ninety percent of our audience say the same thing," she told him in a congratulatory tone.

"But I'm telling you right now that it's not going to happen," said Malcolm in exasperation.

"I wouldn't put any money on it yet," said Lois pragmatically. "These polls change by the hour. We could have a complete turnaround by tomorrow."

"SO, ANY SPARKS FLYING?"

Jessie tilted her head quizzically. Lois had already taken

Malcolm aside for a tête-à-tête and now it was Jessie's turn. "Sparks?" she asked.

Lois smiled encouragingly. "With the others. How are you all getting along?"

"Pretty good, I guess. We're still getting to know each other."

Lois brought the clipboard up to her chest and folded her arms across it, leaning forward slightly. "And Nick? How are you getting on with him?"

Jessie shrugged. "He's great. He really knows his stuff. We're all having a lot of fun."

She looked at Lois who was nodding slowly, her eyes unreadable behind the dark glasses.

"Right," said Lois. "Sure." She waved a hand at their surroundings. "Being on an island like this...thrown together by circumstance...it must bring up some strong feelings."

Jessie didn't really know what to say.

"Feelings that generally remain dormant in our everyday, civilized lives. Primal feelings, as it were." Lois paused meaningfully. "Urges."

Jessie blinked and felt a blush rising in her cheeks. She didn't know where to look.

"Yes," continued Lois, "I bet there are lots of primal urges coming to the surface." She leaned forward and lowered her voice conspiratorially. "It's only natural, you know. A man, a woman, the sultry heat of the Tropics. Don't be afraid of those feelings, that's all I'm saying. In fact, you should feel free to act on them."

Jessie was dumbstruck with embarrassment. And she couldn't help wondering what Lois had told Malcolm.

"I hadn't really thought about it," she told Lois at last. "I guess we're all too busy dealing with the survival stuff." She attempted a joke. "You should probably be grateful that we're not at each other's throats by now."

There was a pause and Lois's face turned speculative. Tilting the clipboard she made a quick note while she talked. "That is another way to go, but I'm going to leave it on ice for the moment. I'll let you know."

She brought the clipboard back to her chest. "Any questions you want to ask me?" she asked in a tone that suggested that the answer to her question contained only two letters.

Jessie shook her head, only too eager to get away.

"Great," said Lois. "Send Cindi over to me, would you?"

Jessie went back to the others and busied herself with making some minor repairs to her shoes but she couldn't help looking up every so often at Cindi and Lois, who were giggling like sorority sisters.

"So, what was that about?" asked Nick, as he passed on his way to the beach. "Did she give you a pep talk?"

Jessie smiled wanly. "Sort of."

NICK, NICK, NICK.

Jessie walked on, trying to jog her brain out of its rut, trying desperately to shift her thoughts from the one thing they always came back to.

She paused and made a quick detour as she spotted a flash of red among the green. She struggled past some knotted vines and examined the red and pink leaves of the shrub, checking her list. Could this be a copperleaf plant? She shrugged, picking it and adding it to the other things in her bag.

Nick had sent them off on a scavenger hunt, armed only with a list, a whistle and a cloth bag. There were fifteen things on the list and the first person to return with any ten would win.

Secretly, Jessie wasn't trying too hard. It seemed like yesterday's accusation of cheating had been forgotten but Jessie had decided that she wouldn't mind if today's point went to someone else. She was more interested in using the time to explore some unknown parts of the island and she was currently about halfway up a small mountain that she'd found inland on the northeast side. She planned to wander around for a couple of hours and would pick up stuff if she found it along the way.

She had also planned to think about other things besides Nick, but her brain was being singularly unaccommodating about that. At the moment she was trying to get rid of a mental picture of him arguing with Malcolm the night before. Something about football. Malcolm had been squawking in indignation and Nick had been passionate as they both grew more heated in the defense of their teams.

Jessie blinked self-consciously as she realized she was grinning to herself on camera. Lois would just love that.

With a final burst of effort she reached the top of the slope and gasped as she took in the full wonder of the view. The island stretched out in all directions below her. To the south she could see the long, golden stretch of the beach and, squinting, she imagined she could make out their shelters. Looking to her right she caught a glint of blue from the lagoon, hidden well in its glade of trees. Far out to sea she could see the anchored yacht, looking like a toy on the surface of the water.

Jessie walked along the ridge until she came to a tall pandanus tree, birds squawking in the leafy heights. She sat down, resting her back against the trunk and took a long drink of water from the bottle she'd brought with her. She let her gaze wander and realized she was smiling again but didn't bother trying to quash it. It was a glorious day. She was tanned and healthy and relatively well fed. Who wouldn't be smiling?

She sighed with pleasure and made a mental note to thank Nick for sending them on this scavenger hunt.

Nick.

Hard as she tried to distract herself, her thoughts always came back to him. There was no getting away from it—she had a full-blown, helpless crush on him. The more she tried to ignore it, the worse it got. She admired him, she felt good around him and she was agonizingly attracted to him. When she looked into his eyes it was like everything stopped and they were the only two people in the world.

And, the strange thing was, that there were moments when she could swear that the attraction was mutual. But what if she was only imagining it?

That was the trouble with attraction, it turned your judgment to mush.

Not that she was exactly an expert when it came to men and their feelings anyway. Just look at how she'd misread Tom for instance. She'd had absolutely no idea what *he'd* been thinking.

The memory irked her and she got up restlessly, heading down the other side of the ridge, towards some coconut trees she'd spotted in the distance.

Even if Nick does like you, she asked herself, what difference does it make? It's not like you can seduce him on national television. What kind of a person would do something like that?

Cindi with two *i*s would do it, came the unbidden thought.

"Well, I wouldn't," muttered Jessie firmly. Then she ducked her head and pressed her lips together. Smiling on camera was one thing but she really should draw the line at talking to herself.

JESSIE STOOD AT THE BASE OF the tree and stared up at the coconuts which were yellow and cylindrical.

She looked down and checked the list again. Nope, bananas definitely weren't on it. She sighed and then tilted her head back, gazing up at the flamboyant starburst of leaves and the enticing yellow bounty.

Why shouldn't she get them anyway? She didn't care about the challenge, may as well bring back some food.

She pressed her palms against the trunk and pushed. Nothing. Then she wrapped her arms halfway around the trunk and jiggled back and forth. Even less effect. She looked up again.

It sure was a tall tree.

Jessie narrowed her eyes in determination and then she searched the surrounding area. All thoughts of the scavenger hunt had been pushed out by this new challenge.

She was going to get those bananas.

She found a couple of strong vines and wound them together to form a harness, like she'd seen Nick make in a program the previous year, then she took off her shoes and wrapped the vine around the tree, forming a loose loop. She leaned back from the trunk until the vine was taut and she braced one foot against the trunk. This was the tricky part. She took a breath and quickly brought up her other foot, using the flexion in her knees to keep the vine taut enough to hold her weight.

She bent her knees slightly and, as the vine loosened, she rapidly slid it up the trunk, bracing herself again before she could drop. She walked a couple of steps up the trunk and then bent her knees, sliding the rope up again.

She repeated the movement again and again, incredulous that it was actually working.

Her legs were just beginning to give out when she reached the top. With all the grace of a newborn foal she clambered onto one of the branches, sweat popping out on her brow as she fell across it. After a moment she sat up and began to laugh with triumphant exuberance as she gazed around, marveling at the situation she found herself in. She really hoped the Island Eyes were picking up every moment of this. She would have to watch the tape herself just to prove she didn't dream it.

Humming to herself with unfettered happiness she began to work on the bananas, pulling them off one by one and throwing them down, hoping they wouldn't be too bruised by the fall. Not that they wouldn't eat them anyway.

The last one she peeled and ate with a pleasure that bordered on indecent.

For the first time in years Jessie Banks was experiencing something other than quiet satisfaction in her work and quiet contentment with her life. She was feeling exhilaration, fear, exhaustion, discomfort, excitement, triumph and exasperation. They weren't all good feelings but they were *new*—and she was reveling in them.

She sat for a while longer and then decided that she had to climb down, before the prospect became too daunting. She had an uneasy feeling that descent was going to be harder than coming up had been.

She was just about to climb off her perch when she heard a rustling sound, coming from below. She hesitated and looked around, peering at the surrounding bushes and undergrowth.

"Nick?" she called doubtfully, wondering if she'd been away longer than she'd thought.

There was another, more violent rustle and Jessie's attention focused on a bush with trembling leaves.

"Nick?" she repeated warily. "Is that you?"

The bush shook again and Jessie gasped as a large, brown pig emerged. Its back was bristling and long tusks swept the air as its head swung around, searching. Jessie's gasp turned into an exclamation of delight as the pig was followed closely by a roly-poly bunch of pink piglets, all squealing and tumbling over each other in their rush to keep up.

Jessie watched them with increasing amusement. It was hard to believe that such cute little piglets would grow up to be great, lumbering beasts like their mother.

Then her smile slowly faded and her eyebrows dipped down into a frown. The pig family had found her scattered bananas and were beginning to root around among them.

"Hey, wait just a minute," said Jessie.

They didn't pay any attention to her and Jessie's eyes widened as she watched mommy pig scoff down a whole banana in one go.

"Hey!" called Jessie in outrage. "Those are mine! Get away from them!" She looped the sling around herself again and began her descent, yelling at the pigs.

She was about one-third of the way down when it slowly dawned on her that mommy pig was actually quite a large animal.

She hesitated. The piglets had followed their mother's lead and were now attacking the fruit with enthusiasm, little jaws working frantically.

"Stop that!" Jessie tried yelling again.

This time mommy pig did notice her. She lifted her head, fixed a beady eye on Jessie and snarled a warning.

Jessie recoiled in surprise. Whoa, she thought, what big tusks you have.

She inched down a little farther and tried to yell out with a confidence that was fast dissipating.

"Hey, there, pigs—shoo! Get lost!"

There was a much bigger snarl.

Jessie climbed rapidly back up to her safe branch.

"Fine," she muttered angrily. "Have the bananas, be my guests."

She watched hopelessly as the pigs made a meal of the

fruit, wondering whether anyone would believe her. As an excuse this ranked right up there with "the dog ate my homework."

She hoped fervently that the cameras were catching all this. They probably were. In fact, people were probably having a good laugh at her right now, her hard-won fruit being scoffed up by a family of wild pigs.

She peered down at the grunting, snuffling animals.

Or were they boars?

Whatever they were, they finished up the bananas and played for a little while, chasing each other and mock fighting. Jessie smiled reluctantly, charmed despite herself.

Then the mother collapsed onto her side at the base of the tree and the piglets came scrambling up to her, squealing with delight. Jessie couldn't help laughing. One by one, the piglets settled down, curling up next to their mother's huge body and falling asleep.

Finally, thought Jessie as she rubbed a cramp out of her thigh muscle, I can get out of here.

She waited for a few minutes after the mother pig closed her eyes and, once again, started the climb down. This time she made it halfway before mommy's eyes flicked open and she lifted her heavy head, pinning Jessie with a fierce stare.

Jessie ventured a little farther and the pig's mouth curled up. Not only did she have tusks, she also had very sharp teeth.

Jessie went back up and collapsed across the tree branch with a plaintive cry of exasperation.

An hour passed and Jessie no longer knew whether she was feeling tired, bored or just plain stupid. The pigs were showing absolutely no sign of moving and she had no idea what to do. Her stomach was growling with hunger and all she could do was curse her efficiency in throwing down every single banana from the tree.

For crying out loud, she thought, where are the Island Eyes when I need them. Can't anybody see me up here?

"Hello?" she called out, feeling ridiculous. "Can anybody hear me?"

She paused. "Nick? Kenny?" She looked down at the pigs who were utterly undisturbed by her shouting.

"Lois?" she called into the emptiness. "Anyone?"

"I *HAD A FEATHER!*" said Malcolm as he turned his bag inside out and shook it. "I swear!" He looked suspiciously at Cindi's bounty. "Did you take my feather?"

Cindi curled her hand protectively around her stash. "No, I didn't take your stupid feather. Go away."

Nick looked at the camera with a deadpan expression. "I am marooned on this island with a bunch of ten-year-olds." He turned towards the contestants. "Malcolm, feather or not, here I come."

"...7-8-9-10," said Cindi, counting out her booty yet again. She fired a smug look at Malcolm. A vein pulsed in his forehead as he scanned the surrounding area.

Nick looked through Cindi's haul, trying not to show his amazement. He hadn't expected her to come back with anything on the list and here she was with ten. He went over to Malcolm and sifted through his items. Unfortunately, he was definitely missing a feather, leaving his grand total at nine.

"Sorry, Malcolm," said Nick. "Cindi's won it."

Cindi squealed and Nick felt himself rocked on his feet as she threw her arms around his neck.

"I can't believe it," she shrieked. "I won, I won. Thank you." She wrapped her legs around his waist like an overeager monkey and planted her lips against his cheek.

Nick could hear Kenny's suppressed snorts of laughter and he put his hands on Cindi's waist and tried to pry her off.

"Okay," he said. "Congratulations. Well done. Er, why don't you shake hands with Malcolm and show that there's no hard feelings?"

He finally managed to get Cindi back on her feet and she raced off to boast to the confession cam.

Nick looked up along the length of the beach. "You didn't happen to see Jessie at all in your travels, did you?"

Malcolm shook his head, looking utterly dejected by his failure to win the scavenger hunt.

Nick shrugged. "We'll give her some time." He clapped Malcolm encouragingly on the shoulder. "Meanwhile, you and I can get started on building a raft. Lois may not let me set these things as challenges, but they still have to be done." Malcolm brightened and Nick dispatched him to the forest to collect sticks.

"We'll do this as a piece-to-camera," Nick instructed Kenny, "as soon as I've braided some rope."

Kenny started to make some adjustments to the camera and Nick tore thin strips off a length of vine.

"I like her," said Kenny conversationally.

"Cindi?" said Nick.

Kenny laughed. "God, no. She's a nutcase. I mean Jessie. She's nice."

Nick brushed his sleeve across his face, wiping off the sweat and sand. "Yeah, I guess she is," he said absently.

"She's got guts," expanded Kenny. "And, no matter what happens, she manages to keep her sense of humor. You notice that?"

Nick started to plait the strips of vine into a rope. "Sure," he said. "She's doing great. You know what, you should probably get some tape of me doing this after all." He looked into the camera and waited for Kenny to start rolling, but Kenny, for once, seemed to be in a talkative mood.

"You guys work well together, too."

Nick looked at the cameraman for a moment. He frowned slightly, then shrugged. "I guess so."

Kenny nodded sagely. "Yeah, you look good with each other. Comfortable, you know?"

Nick's perplexed expression suddenly cleared. "Oh, okay. How much is she paying you?"

"Jessie?"

"No," Nick scolded. "Lois. How much is she giving you to try and stir things up?"

Kenny shook his head. "Don't know what you mean. I was just talking."

Nick peered suspiciously at him but Kenny's face was completely clear of guile.

"Oh," said Nick. "Sorry." He returned his attention to the rope but Kenny's next words brought his head up again.

"I'm not sure Lois has even noticed it."

Nick paused carefully. "Noticed what?"

"That you like her," said Kenny, checking the filter lens on the camera.

"What are you talking about?"

Kenny tilted his head. "Oh, come on," he said with a smile. "It's so obvious. Okay, maybe not to Lois but I've been following you around. Me and my camera, we got eyes."

Nick didn't know what to say. He was wondering what exactly Kenny had seen that had led him to this conclusion.

Kenny spoke up as if reading his mind. "Hey, don't worry, it's not like you've been acting out of ordinary on camera. You're the same smooth professional as always. But I've been your shadow for almost two years and I'm telling you, I am seeing a side of you that I've never seen before. You're flirting, man."

Nick was embarrassed at being found so transparent and worried that Jessie might have noticed it, too. "Maybe you've just got a thing for her yourself."

Kenny laughed again. "Well, besides the fact that she's way out of my league, she's not exactly my type."

Nick smiled wryly. He'd met some of Kenny's girlfriends and they all looked the same to him, decorated as they were with myriad piercings and tattoos.

He looked down at the rope again and thought about what Kenny was saying. "Maybe we should just get on with this raft-building."

Kenny gave an easygoing shrug. "Hey, I'm ready to roll." He slipped on his headphones and tucked his head behind the camera. The recording light blinked on.

Nick opened his mouth to start but then he turned his head towards the forest and a faraway look came into his eyes. After a moment he turned back to the camera.

"Did you hear that?"

Without waiting for an answer he turned away again and narrowed his eyes in concentration.

"There," he said. "Did you hear it?"

Kenny lowered his headphones. "All I can hear," he said apologetically, "is your voice asking me if I can hear anything."

"It's an SOS," said Nick urgently. "Drop the camera, let's go."

Kenny hesitated, looking anguished. "You know I can't. Lois will have my job."

Nick nodded. "Okay, come on anyway. Follow me as best you can."

He turned and struck out across the sand, each long stride taking him farther away from Kenny. He almost crashed into Malcolm as they met at the edge of the forest.

"Stay here," Nick instructed, heading into the trees. He ran quickly, stopping every so often to try and hear where the SOS was coming from.

At least the fact that she was sending out a signal meant

that she was alive. Maybe she was injured or maybe, he dared to hope, she was just stranded.

He ran on through the forest, changing direction as the piercing whistle faded or became louder. He was still some way off from the banana trees, struggling through neck-high bushes when he heard her pausing in her whistle-blowing to call for help.

"Jessie," he yelled. "I'm coming."

A movement in one of the trees caught his eye and as he moved closer he saw Jessie waving at him. It felt like a huge weight being lifted off his chest.

"Nick," she called with plaintive relief. "I'm so glad you're here."

He grinned, still ploughing through the bushes. "What's the matter?" he teased. "Don't tell me you can't climb down."

Her voice floated down to him as she pointed towards the base of the tree. "I'm trapped. By wild—"

Nick missed the last word. He slowed in his approach, moving more warily. Out of force of habit he took out his hunting knife.

He approached cautiously and parted the last veil of bushes to see Jessie's hostage-takers.

He looked up at her. "Pigs?" he said quietly, in disbelief.

"Are you sure they aren't boars?" she asked.

"They're definitely pigs," he said with a smile. He looked back down at the cozy family, dozing about thirty feet from where he was standing. "And I hate to break it to you, but they're fast asleep."

"Only because I'm sitting on this branch," she said with a hint of asperity. "Believe me, the minute I try to come down, they'll wake up. Well, mommy pig will anyway."

"That's a good idea," said Nick. "Can you do that, to distract her?"

He stepped silently out of the bushes and started inching towards the pig and her brood.

"Wait a minute," said Jessie. "Is that a knife?"

Nick stopped and tilted his head back. "Yeah. Good for you, you got us dinner." He glanced watchfully at the pigs and then back up at Jessie who was looking upset.

"No," she said. "You can't."

"What?"

"You can't. She was only protecting her young."

Nick looked at the pigs again. The mother was snuffling as she started to wake and Nick spoke quickly.

"It's okay," he explained. "We'll only take the adult. The piglets will be fine, they're weaned. They're about eight weeks old, they'll be able to forage for themselves."

"Please, Nick," begged Jessie. "Don't hurt her. There's bound to be others, without family."

The animal in question let out another sleepy snort and her eyes flickered open. If a pig could look surprised, this one did. She squealed and scrambled to her feet, rousing her young ones and chasing them into the bush, away from Nick. She then turned and planted her feet, squaring off against him. But when he made no threatening move, she turned quickly and trundled after her family.

Nick looked up at Jessie again, spreading his arms in a display of his compliance. He was pleased by her answering smile.

He walked over and dug with his toe among the scattered remains of the bananas as Jessie climbed down.

"Did they eat them all?" she asked in a forlorn voice as she reached the ground.

"I'm afraid so," said Nick. "Never mind, we'll chalk it up to experience."

Jessie put her hand up against the tree trunk and Nick looked over, suddenly noticing how pale she was.

"Are you okay?" he said, stepping towards her.

"My legs are a bit wobbly," she confessed with a shaky laugh. "I thought I was going to be up there all night." She held a hand up in front of her face. "I can't believe this, I'm trembling."

"Come here," said Nick. He put his arms around her, enveloping her in a strong hug. She let out a long, grateful sigh and Nick held her, rubbing her back as her tremors eased off.

"Thanks," she mumbled into his chest. "I guess I'm not as tough as I thought I was."

He smiled, looking down at her head. "Hey, the thought of spending a night in a banana tree would upset anyone. Besides, it looks like you were doing really well until those pigs showed up."

He felt her giggle in response. "I was," she insisted firmly. Her arms tightened around his waist. "Thank you for coming to rescue me." The words were slightly muffled against his chest.

"My pleasure," he said. "I love having the chance to act like a hero."

Another giggle from her. She lifted her head and looked at him. Her eyes were a dark, glowing brown and they grew serious as he looked into them. Neither of them spoke and, when she didn't let go of him, Nick lowered his head towards hers.

She lifted her face and their lips met in a soft kiss. Nick closed his eyes and felt fireworks going off in his head. All the confusion and wonderings about his feelings disappeared as he kissed her. He only wanted it to go on and on. He tightened his arms around her as her arms encircled his neck. He felt goose bumps spring up as her hand brushed the back of his neck and her fingers entwined in his hair.

"Nick?" came a plaintive cry from the bush, bringing him sharply back to reality "Can you hear me? I don't know where I am. Hello?"

ON THE WALK BACK TO CAMP Jessie was grateful that she had a tale of adventure to relate to Kenny, something to explain her flushed face and hyperactive excitement. She spoke in excited bursts over her shoulder while Nick led the way, not looking back at them at all.

Even as her mouth was forming the words—Tusks! Piglets! Incredible height! Terrified!—her brain was completely absorbed with the kiss and whether it had been caught on the Island Eyes and what it meant for them if it had.

And what it meant anyway.

They reached the camp and Jessie had to start again, telling the story to the others. Her lips were still tingling with the memory of the kiss and her heart thudded erratically every time she looked at Nick.

During it all, he said little, just the odd comment about his part in the rescue.

There was an awkward moment when Malcolm harangued them for not bringing back a pig. Jessie thought Nick was going to expose her sentimentality, which she was feeling increasingly foolish about, but he just said that the piglets hadn't looked weaned. Jessie glanced at him, hoping to share a grateful and meaningful look, but he didn't look at her.

She decided he was being wise. She was sure that the electricity between them was almost palpable. She could feel it in the very air around them. The secret knowledge and their shared complicity in not mentioning it, pervaded everything they said or did.

Cindi and Malcolm were further disappointed when Jessie told them that none of the bananas had survived the pigs' appetites. At least, thought Jessie practically, her abysmal failure today was putting her back on par with the other contestants.

She felt a spark of hilarity in her brain. If they wanted to make accusations of favoritism now she had the perfect example for them.

"So you didn't get anything at all?" said Cindi. "Not even from the scavenger hunt list?"

Jessie remembered her bag and emptied out her paltry scraps. "Uh, a tern feather, a copperleaf branch and a piece of bamboo."

"So I'm still the winner?" said Cindi, warily hopeful.

Nick nodded, smiling at her. Cindi shouted in triumph, bounced around a few times with her hands in the air and then enveloped Nick in a hug.

Jessie looked away and smothered a smile, feeling so sorry for Cindi and her blatant, futile flirting.

Until Malcolm spoke.

"Here we go again," he muttered in a weary undertone.

Jessie looked sharply at him and then back at Cindi and Nick. They were laughing and his hands were on her tiny waist. Jessie's stomach turned over and she got a tinny taste in her mouth.

What was Malcolm talking about?

NICK COULDN'T SLEEP. He'd been tossing and turning for over an hour and he was no closer to getting Jessie out of his head.

Kissing her had been a huge mistake.

It had happened so quickly. He'd found her in his arms and he hadn't even thought twice about it, just given in to the irresistible urge.

For such a bad idea, it had been a great kiss. Warm and passionate, firing him up from the inside in an instant. Even thinking about it again made his heart speed up pleasantly.

He still didn't know why he'd done it. Okay, obviously he was attracted to her but he didn't want to start anything, not like this anyway.

He'd been painfully on edge for the rest of the day, not knowing what he'd say if she tried to corner him about it or, even worse, if she told the others about it. It was so uncharacteristic of him and an image as some kind of Casanova was the last thing he wanted linked to his name or his show.

But she hadn't said anything and, as the evening progressed, that struck him as somewhat calculating. He started to worry about her motivations. Was it possible that she'd done it somehow to get an edge in the competition, a bit of salaciousness that she could bring out later to up her ratings?

Nick turned over again, flattening down an uncomfortable lump in his bed.

It just would have been so much better if it had never happened.

6

IT HADN'T TAKEN Jessie long to figure out that something was wrong. From the moment she'd emerged from her shelter that morning she hadn't been alone with Nick for one second.

In fact, looking back, she hadn't been alone with him since they'd kissed.

Back at camp, after the thrill of her rescue had died down, Nick had returned to the task of building a raft. He'd talked directly to the camera as he'd done it, taking the audience through it step-by-step. Jessie, Cindi and Malcolm had taken turns at helping, in between stints at the confession cam or catching up on the daily chores: gathering firewood, purifying water, refreshing their flattened bedding, patching holes in the shelters.

As the evening progressed Nick had continued to act like nothing had happened and Jessie had grown more subdued as the thrill of the kiss gradually wore off, to be replaced by a confused uneasiness which was only exacerbated by the flirty rapport he seemed to have with Cindi.

Jessie hadn't slept well and she'd been glad when the morning had come. Objectively, Nick was treating her much the same as the others. A cheerful "good morning," jokes about the weather and Malcolm's snoring and teasing them about the upcoming challenge. But it felt to Jessie as if he was operating on autopilot and her attempts to make eye contact were unequivocally ignored.

After breakfast Nick led them on a short trek to the north beach where the elves from the yacht had been hard at work again.

The contestants stopped dead in their tracks, amazed by the spectacle in front of them. Spanning the beach for almost a mile was a breathtaking obstacle course. Rope-ladders, wooden bridges, intricate mazes, platforms, systems of weights and pulleys, mud pits, moats, tunnels, nets, walls and fences. It was like a cross between an army assault course and a fantasy labyrinth created by a child.

A rather demented child.

Nick smiled at their expressions and handed each of them a key with a ribbon on it. Malcolm's was green, Cindi's red and Jessie's ribbon was blue.

"There are small locked boxes hidden around this course," explained Nick. "Twenty-one altogether. That means seven each. The boxes are numbered and the locks are colored red, green or blue. The key you're holding opens the first and the key in there opens the second and so on."

He smiled at each of them, once again managing to do it without meeting Jessie's eyes. "You'll probably find the boxes out of sequence so it'll help if you try and remember where you saw them. If you find someone else's box you can just ignore it." He lifted an eyebrow and spoke ironically. "Or you can tell each other where those boxes are."

He nodded in wry acknowledgment as they chuckled. "There's no time limit. First one to reach his or her last box and give me what's inside, wins. There's also food and water in some of the boxes because, take my word for it, we're going to be here all day. Okay, off you go. Good luck."

AN HOUR HAD PASSED and Jessie was on her third box. The sun was high in the sky and she was sitting in the shade of a wooden platform, sipping gratefully at the bottle of water she'd found.

The course was absolutely devilish. The boxes were small and hard to find and she'd spent a lot of her time climbing up rickety ladders or wading through swampy mud pits only to find that the lock on the box was green or red. At least it was happening to the others, too. The first time Cindi had found a useless box she'd let out a cry of disappointment, only to have both Malcolm and Jessie make a beeline for her. It had turned out to be one of Malcolm's. But Jessie had learned. Now when she found a useless box she kept quiet, or even pretended to open it, and she always kept one eye on Malcolm and Cindi.

Trying to spot new boxes, trying to figure out the easiest way to tackle obstacles, trying to remember where she'd spotted one of her other boxes: Jessie would really have been enjoying it if she wasn't still plagued by the nagging infuriation with Nick. Why on earth had he kissed her if he was just going to pretend it hadn't happened?

She finished the water and started the next leg. She had already come across blue box number four, but she couldn't remember if it had been at the top of the log pyramid or if it was in the middle of the raised-platform maze.

The maze was nearest.

Except that to get there she had to walk past Cindi, who was sitting at the opening of a series of pipe tunnels, and Nick, who was standing with folded arms and an amused expression on his face.

Jessie was aggravated to feel her stomach quiver with nervousness as she approached them.

"I'll give you five thousand dollars," said Cindi. "Come on, everyone's got their price. Just tell me yours and we can cut to the chase."

Play the Lucky Hearts Game

and get...

2 FREE BOOKS
and a FREE MYSTERY GIFT...

yes! YOURS to KEEP!

I have scratched off the silver card, Please send me my *2 FREE BOOKS* and *FREE mystery GIFT*. I understand that I am under no obligation to purchase any books as explained on the back of this card.

Scratch Here!
then look below to see
what your cards get you...
2 Free Books & a Free
Mystery Gift!

---

331 HDL DU64

131 HDL DU7L

FIRST NAME	LAST NAME

ADDRESS

APT.#	CITY

STATE/PROV.	ZIP/POSTAL CODE

(H-F-10/03)

Twenty-one gets you
2 FREE BOOKS
and a *FREE MYSTERY GIFT!*

Twenty gets you
2 FREE BOOKS!

Nineteen gets you
1 FREE BOOK!

TRY AGAIN!

Offer limited to one per household and not valid to current Harlequin Flipside™ subscribers. All orders subject to approval.

▶ DETACH AND MAIL CARD TODAY! ▶

BUSINESS REPLY MAIL

FIRST-CLASS MAIL   PERMIT NO. 717-003   BUFFALO, NY

POSTAGE WILL BE PAID BY ADDRESSEE

HARLEQUIN READER SERVICE
3010 WALDEN AVE
PO BOX 1867
BUFFALO NY 14240-9952

NO POSTAGE
NECESSARY
IF MAILED
IN THE
UNITED STATES

Nick cocked his head. "But what happens if I agree and then you don't win?"

"But I *am* going to win," argued Cindi. "Okay, I'll give you ten thousand. How about it?"

"For one box?" said Nick, as if he was seriously considering it.

Jessie wanted to walk straight past but she knew it would look odd, so she stopped, carefully equidistant from both of them. "You're actually trying to bribe him?" she asked Cindi. "With money you don't even have?"

Cindi smiled winsomely. "I don't like small spaces. Hey, will you go in and tell me if there's a box in there? I'll give you five thousand dollars."

Jessie laughed at her cheek. Impulsively, she grinned at Nick. "I heard her offering you ten. I think I should hold out."

Nick, who had been sparring so cheerfully with Cindi, responded to Jessie's banter with a polite laugh as his eyes followed Malcolm.

Jessie felt stung to the quick. Her face flushed and she dug her fingernails into her palm.

Nick looked back at her, his expression as bland as if he'd never met her before. "Are you getting on okay?" he said. "Do you need any help? I can't give you any hints but if you want any practical advice—"

"No." She cut him off. "I don't want any practical advice." Her words came in staccato bursts, like fat spitting off a grill. "Thanks though. Thanks a lot."

She stormed off, determination to win this challenge running through her veins like molten lava. What on earth was his problem? Just because he'd kissed her, did that give him the right to suddenly start treating her *worse* than the others? What was he so afraid of? That his kiss was so potent that she was going to fall head-over-heels and beg him to marry her or something? Is that what all the leave-me-alone warning signs were about?

Talk about an ego. Did he seriously think she'd come on this trip just to meet him? How big-headed was that?

Boy, she was going to finish this course without his help *and* she was going to win the million and then she'd…she'd buy out his program and fire him!

Okay, that was a little psychotic. She wouldn't do that, but she would win this challenge.

JESSIE SETTLED HERSELF on the seat in front of the confession cam and shook her hair back from her face. For such a simple thing, getting shampoo really had made a huge difference.

"Hi, everyone," she said. She smiled. Talking to the camera no longer felt so strange. "I'm finding it hard to believe that this is only day five. I feel like I've been here for weeks.

"The producer, Lois, told us yesterday about the great response we're getting on the Web site. I have to be honest, it is freaking me out a bit. I mean, I knew in theory that we were on camera, but I guess it's only dawning on me now that there are people watching it all."

Jessie laughed. "And not just my friends! Who I know at least will be kind." She made a wry face. "That obstacle course was harder than it looked, okay? And he only beat me by seconds!"

She laughed again. "Okay, I admit it, Malcolm won it fair and square. Let's see, what's the score now? Don't quote me on this but I think Malcolm and I are two and Cindi is one. Oh, you know what? It's probably up on the Web site anyway."

She paused, then smiled. "I am really going to sleep tonight. I must say, sleeping in general has become easier. I'm getting used to the sounds of the island. The wind in the trees, the sound of the waves, even the odd screeches of birds—these all seem kind of friendly to me now."

Jessie looked down, chewing at her lip. Okay, so she hadn't slept too well the night before but she wasn't planning to talk about that. She felt a sudden wave of loneliness. It would be so great to sit down with one of her girlfriends and analyze what had happened with Nick. So much easier than turning it over and over in her own head.

She looked up again, understanding the meaning of the phrase "put on a brave face."

"I'm definitely going to win the challenge tomorrow," she grinned. "Whatever it is. I'm determined! So you can log on to the Web site and put money on it."

She heard what she'd said and tried hastily to take it back. "Not large amounts of money. In fact, don't put money on it at all because I don't know if I'm going to win or not. I'm hoping I'll win and I'm using a positive attitude, but that's not to be confused with a guarantee."

She put her hands on her hips and leaned forward. "I'm talking to you in particular, Granddad. You stick to losing money on the horses."

She paused, picturing her grandfather's face, creased with laugh lines. The loneliness jabbed at her again and she swallowed as a lump rose in her throat.

"Anyway, I'll say good-night to you all again and I'll go and have some dinner." She clasped her hands in front of her chest in mock excitement. "I can't wait to see what surprises are on the menu tonight. Ooh, I hope it's fish!"

"I WENT UP THAT STUPID pyramid three times," grumbled Cindi, rubbing at her calves. "My legs are killing me."

Jessie frowned. "It was a blue box at the top of the pyramid. One of mine."

"I know!" screeched Cindi. "I got mixed up and confused

the pyramid with that spiderweb thingy, you know, with the poles?"

Jessie nodded in understanding. The postmortem discussion of the obstacle course was proving great fun. They'd finished dinner a couple of hours before, Kenny had returned to the yacht and, as the night fell, the fireside conversation was still dominated by tales of obstacle-course bravado.

As Malcolm and Cindi argued amiably about which had been worse, the mud pits or the tunnels, Jessie watched their faces in the flickering firelight. Even though it had only been five days, Malcolm's had grown leaner and his deepening tan suited him. The smudges of dirt on Cindi's neck and the light scratches on her arms somehow added a humanizing effect.

Jessie avoided looking at Nick. She knew all too well what he was like. Good-looking, affable, convivial yet self-contained, infuriating and annoying.

Malcolm yawned, stretching. "Man, I'll sleep tonight."

"Oh," said Nick, looking chagrined.

"What?" said Malcolm.

"I was planning to take you all night-fishing," said Nick. "The tide's out so we could go out to the sandbank beyond the cliffs. I thought it might be something different."

The contestants avoided his eyes, nobody looking too thrilled by the prospect.

"Is it a challenge?" said Cindi at last.

"Uh, no," said Nick. "I just thought it might be fun for you."

Cindi looked hugely relieved. "You know what, in that case I think I'll give it a miss."

"Me, too," said Malcolm, standing up as if he was afraid that Nick was going to physically drag him down to the water. "I'm kind of wiped out after winning the challenge today." He put on an extremely modest face, then put up his hands as Cindi and Jessie threw bits of papaya skin at him.

"Okay, okay," he surrendered, laughing. "I was just kidding around." He looked worried. "I hope I didn't come off as too cocky when I talked about it in the confession cam."

Cindi wailed, slapping her forehead. "Oh, no, I forgot to do the confession cam." Her shoulders slumped wearily at the thought of it. "Maybe Lois wouldn't mind if I didn't do it for one night." She smiled at their expressions. "Yeah, I know," she said, dragging herself to her feet. "Okay, but I'm going straight to bed after it. See you guys in the morning."

All good things come to those who wait, thought Jessie, watching with satisfaction as Malcolm and Cindi left.

She turned to Nick and raised her eyebrows expectantly.

"Maybe we should leave it," said Nick. "And wait for a night when everyone can come."

"Oh, no," Jessie said firmly. "We're doing this tonight."

"...AND THE BRIGHTEST STARS in the constellation Gemini are called Castor and Pollux, who were twin deities who helped shipwrecked sailors."

Jessie wasn't looking at the stars. She was glaring at the side of Nick's face.

"Really?" she said, not bothering to disguise the sarcasm in her voice. "That's fascinating."

They were standing thigh-deep in warm, moonlit water, fishing lines held out in front of them and Nick seemed determined to regale her with the mythological background of every single constellation in the inky-black sky.

Jessie wasn't sure if they were still on camera, but they had taken off their microphones at the shore so she knew they couldn't be heard. Oh, the poor audience, she thought sardonically, missing out on this riveting monologue.

Nick paused, his eyes still firmly fixed to the sky, and Jessie cut in quickly.

"Look," she said brightly, pointing at a random spot in the heavens. "That constellation is called 'The Castaways.' Do you know that story?" Without waiting for an answer she launched into it.

"Yes, it's a very sad story about a maiden and a handsome man who were stranded on a desert island. Time passed until one day they found themselves under a banana tree where they kissed."

Jessie could feel Nick standing very still beside her and she went on, warming to her theme.

"Unfortunately, it was an enchanted banana tree, so while the maiden knew that the kiss had happened, apparently the man had absolutely no memory of it at all."

Jessie sighed expressively. "The gods took pity on the maiden and immortalized her in the heavens, all beautiful and twinkly, whereas, sadly, the man was left alone on the island to grow old and wither away."

There was a long silence.

At last Nick spoke. "I'm sorry."

Jessie let out the breath she'd been holding, awash with relief that they were talking about it at last.

"It shouldn't have happened."

Jessie's heart plummeted. She was stunned by how much that sentence hurt. Actually, physically hurt.

"I just acted on impulse," Nick went on. He glanced at her, then away again. "I think we both did."

Jessie was dazed. "Impulse," she said dully.

"Yeah," said Nick. "I think we both just got caught up in the romance of the situation. You were tired and a bit scared from being trapped in the tree and I'd got a fright because I thought you were in danger. It was just a very emotional moment. Don't you think so?"

Jessie swallowed. "Absolutely." Her eyes were stinging and she blinked angrily. "Of course that's what it was. I mean, we hardly know each other."

"Right," said Nick. There was blatant relief in his voice and Jessie's gut knotted.

"But I really am enjoying getting to know you," Nick said in a civil tone. "I think you're doing great. I really admire your spirit and I'm glad you were picked."

"Me, too," said Jessie. Her cheeks were aching with the effort of holding the smile.

Silence descended as they continued to fish. For Jessie it was excruciating. She curled her toes in the gritty sand and tried to ignore the waves which were delicately lapping against her thighs in such a way that it made her think of the one thing she was desperately trying to keep her mind off. She wondered how long she would have to stand here before she could start yawning and making excuses about getting some sleep.

Nick shifted on his feet and Jessie looked up at him, then looked away quickly as she realized he wasn't about to say anything. Another few minutes ticked by. Jessie chewed at the inside of her cheek. The next few days were going to be a nightmare.

She was halfway through her first fake yawn when the fishing rod jerked in her hands. She let out a gasp.

Nick looked at her and then his gaze followed her fishing line to where it entered the water. "Got something?"

"I'm not sure," she said, feeling no further movement. A moment passed and then the rod twitched again.

"Yes," she exclaimed. "That was a tug."

She inched forward a few steps, feeling the sand sucking at her feet and she lifted the rod, reaching out for the line. She caught it on her second try and she started pulling it in slowly, winding it around the protruding hooks on her fishing rod.

"I'm getting really good at this," she joked to Nick, all thoughts of romance momentarily forgotten.

Apparently not so for Nick. He suddenly flung his fishing rod out of his hands and, taking two long strides through the water, wrapped his arms around her.

"Oh, Nick," she cried in surprise, putting one arm around his neck. The other dangled awkwardly, still holding the fishing rod. She closed her eyes and tilted her head for the kiss and then she felt him pull her roughly off her feet. The rod was yanked from her hand and the water beside them erupted in a whoosh of bubbles and spray.

Nick swung her up in one swift movement, catching her legs and holding her above the water. He stood rock still, holding her tightly. Jessie looked around frantically, goose bumps springing out all over her body.

She could feel Nick's heart pounding as his eyes searched the dark water, which had become eerily still.

"Okay," he said at last. "I think he's gone."

Jessie swallowed as she tried to find her voice. "Who?" she croaked.

Nick looked at her, his face shadowed in the moonlight. Drops of water glistened in his hair. When he spoke his voice was calm.

"A gray reef shark." He squeezed her reassuringly as she flinched and then surprised her with a smile. "I think we disturbed him while he was basking. Gave him a free meal though."

Jessie stared at him, her limbs still locked with terror. All she could think about were razor sharp teeth chomping through her leg. One bite, that was all it took. Her leg was stinging at the thought of it.

"Don't put me down," she said suddenly, tightening her hold around Nick's neck.

"Don't worry," he said, laughing gently. He began to walk out of the water while Jessie searched fearfully over his shoulder.

It took a few moments but she eventually realized that her leg actually was stinging. She looked down at it. That wasn't water that was making her calf gleam.

"Oh, no," she cried. "I'm bleeding."

Nick splashed his way out of the water and put her down gently. Jessie scuttled her bottom backwards across the sand, putting a bit more distance between her and the water.

Nick knelt down and examined her leg while Jessie examined his face for any telltale signs that amputation would be required.

"Looks like his tail caught you," said Nick, remarkably cheerfully. "Their skin is like sandpaper. You've got yourself quite a graze."

"A graze?" she said. Wow, talk about death-defying.

"It'll be okay," he said. "We'll wash it with fresh water back at camp."

Jessie dabbed at her leg fretfully and then she looked at Nick whose face was shadowed in the moonlight. She expected him to pull away but he didn't and then she noticed that his brow was still creased and there was anxiety in his eyes.

"Don't look so worried," she said, teasing him gently. "I'll live."

He shook his head and let out a long breath. "You really like getting yourself into trouble, don't you?"

Jessie laughed. "I didn't go looking for it. In fact, technically speaking, *you* got me into trouble that time."

Nick nodded, looking embarrassed. "I think I did. It was

stupid of me to bring you out there, I should have known there was a chance of sharks."

Jessie shrugged. "Great story for the grandkids."

He smiled and met her eyes again.

Jessie felt the blood heating in her veins. His face was so close that she only had to lean forward and they'd be joined in a kiss. Every part of her was aching to touch him.

Nick made the decision for her, tilting forward and cupping her head with his hand as his mouth met hers. The kiss this time was more searching—her lips opened to his immediately and she felt the warmth of his tongue as it probed her mouth. She groaned and then put her hands on his chest, pushing him back.

She wriggled away and jumped up, the pain in her leg forgotten.

"So what's this?" she said, her breath short. "Another *emotional* moment? Don't tell me, we kiss and then it's all back to normal tomorrow?"

She waited as he got to his feet but when he didn't say anything she nodded in bitter recognition.

"I thought so. Well, forget it. I didn't come here just to be a plaything for you."

She turned away and stormed up the beach.

"Jessie, wait a minute."

"Leave me alone," she fired over her shoulder. "You...you *man!*"

7

TALK ABOUT IRONY, thought Jessie. According to Lois, there are approximately a quarter of a million people watching me right now, but can I get Nick to look at me? Of course not.

She cleared her throat again, staring hard at Nick.

"Are you okay?" said Malcolm as he finished off his breakfast. He stood up and came over to look down at her with concern. "You're not feeling feverish are you?"

"No, I'm fine," said Jessie. She kicked her foot hastily over the word she'd written in the sand. "I've just got a frog in my throat."

She looked at Nick again but he was handing a bottle of water over to Kenny. "So what's everyone planning to do today?" he said absently.

"I'm going to try and find that shark," blurted Malcolm. He looked enviously at Jessie's leg. After she'd left Nick, she had washed it off with fresh water and quickly scampered into bed. The large graze was still a bit tender, but Jessie thought it looked worse than it was.

"It'll be gone out to sea again," said Nick kindly. "It's unlikely you'll see him."

"I know," said Malcolm sadly. He took a few steps towards the beach and folded his arms, looking out at the gently rolling waves. Optimism returned to his face. "I'm still going to try."

"My God," said Cindi, rolling her eyes. "What kind of lunatic actively goes looking for a shark?" She yawned hugely, stretching her arms above her head. "I'm still tired," she complained. "I wish you'd told us last night that we were going to have a day off from challenges. I could have slept in."

"I guess that answers my question about what you'll be doing," said Nick.

"I think I'll go to the lagoon again," said Jessie. She stared at Nick, her eyes watering as she willed him to look at her.

Cindi perked up, interested. "Ooh, I'd like to see this famous lagoon. I think I'll go with you."

Jessie thought fast. "That would be fun. I'm going to trek to the north beach first, and then I want to climb the two peaks on the way to the lagoon. We'll have to carry lots of water because the sun will be directly overhead by the time we hit the second one."

"Forget it," said Cindi, slumping back against the tree trunk. "I'll stick to plan A."

Jessie feigned a look of disappointment and then returned to her primary objective.

"Nick?" she said, stretching out her leg. "Could you check the graze for me? Just to make sure it's not infected or anything."

"Sure," he said, coming over and kneeling by her leg.

While he was looking at the wound Jessie wiggled her fingers to get his attention and then pointed to the words she'd traced in the sand.

Lagoon, please.

She watched him read them and then he paused before looking up at her. She widened her eyes. He looked away and she tapped the sand again, prodding the word *please.*

He met her eyes again and then Jessie hurriedly brushed her fingers through the sand as Malcolm came back and dropped to his knees next to them.

"Is it infected?" he asked eagerly. "Do sharks have some

kind of poison in their skin? You know, like a defense mechanism to paralyze their prey? Is it sore? Can I touch it?"

JESSIE WAS PACING by the side of the lagoon when Nick arrived.

"I wasn't sure you'd come," she said shyly.

Nick took off his microphone and he tossed it over next to hers which was lying under a tree. "How's your leg?"

She glanced down at the graze. "It's fine," she said dismissively. "It is just a surface graze." She took a deep breath. In all her pacing she hadn't been able to come up with any preamble so she just blurted it straight out. "I need to know what's going on between us." She paused nervously. "If there *is* anything. You can't just keep kissing me if there's no reason for it... I mean, are you just doing it to kill time or do you...?"

Nick laughed softly. "I'm definitely not doing it to kill time," he said. "I shouldn't be doing it at all but when I'm with you..." He breathed out. "I know I haven't been fair, but this has just caught me completely by surprise." It was his turn to pace. He walked away from her, then turned. Jessie waited, not wanting to interrupt because it seemed like he was gathering his thoughts. He walked back, talking. "I've been fighting this since the first time I saw you. There you were, glaring up at me on the beach. I'd always thought that brown eyes were inevitably soft and kind, but yours were blazing. Then you stood up and I couldn't stop staring at you. Do you have any idea how gorgeous you are?"

Jessie caught her lip between her teeth. "I guess the dress did the trick," she said carefully.

Nick smiled at her. "If that's all it was we wouldn't be having this conversation. That was just the way I felt at the start and I did my utmost to ignore it. As far as I was concerned I was just here to make a show. But the more time I spent with you…" He trailed off, looking at her.

"What?"

He held her eyes. "When I'm with you I find it very hard to think about anything else. You affect the way I see things, the way I act. And I'm trying desperately to hide it from the camera, but I still want to be around you. And at the same time that's a kind of torture because I keep wanting to…" He dipped his head, smiling abashedly. "Well, you know about that. But…"

Jessie waited as the end of the sentence didn't come.

"But?" she said warily.

Nick folded his arms, looking at her with a serious expression. "But I don't really know you. All I know about you is that you've come here to compete for a million dollars and the truth is that I don't know what you'd be willing to do for that."

Jessie stared at him for a moment, then took a step back. She swallowed. "Okay," she said carefully. "You obviously *don't* know me, so I'm going to forget that you said that. Once." She folded her arms, mirroring his defensive stance. "But, since you brought it up, how exactly is seducing you supposed to help me win the money?"

Nick brushed his hand through his hair and grinned at her wryly. "I guess it wouldn't. That was a terrible thing to say. I'm sorry, this whole situation is so artificial and strange." He paused, scratching his chin. "And I think that sometimes people expect more from me when they meet me in real life. They think of me as a TV personality. Then I can see their eyes glazing over when I'm *still* talking about camping or trekking or things like that. But that's what I do, that's who I am. What you see is what you get."

"That's what I like about you," said Jessie, attempting to match his honesty with some of her own. "You love your job so much and your enthusiasm, patience and optimism—they're infectious. And of course I knew I was going to meet 'Nick Garrett' when I came here." She took a deep breath. "And I admit that I was starstruck in the beginning, but that wore off as I got to know you." She laughed at his hurt expression. "To be replaced by something better. And now, when I'm around you I can't think about anything else because I just want to..." She trailed off, smiling at the look he gave her. "As for having a secret agenda, I don't even know why I was picked to be here. I never meant to enter the competition seriously. I mean, I entered it, but my essay was a joke." She peered at him. "Didn't you think that when you read it?"

"I never got to see the essays," said Nick, surprising her. "Lois thought it would be best if I didn't know anything about the contestants before they came here. So, she picked the winners."

Jessie shook her head in amazement. "Well, I still don't know why she picked mine. It was only one sentence long— I can quote it to you." She cleared her throat. "'*My Survival Experience* by Jessie Banks— I've lived in the same one-horse town for my whole life and yet, somehow, I've survived.'"

Nick burst out laughing.

"You see?" exclaimed Jessie. "I never expected to win. I was being sarcastic."

"I dunno," said Nick, still smiling. "I like it."

"Anyway," Jessie went on. "I was stunned when you read my name out and even more so when I got the call from Quest Broadcasting."

"So you just decided, what the heck?"

"Not exactly," said Jessie. She looked at him and made a decision. "Let's sit down."

They went over to the area beside the waterfall; a glade of grass backed by tahinu shrubs and shaded with overhanging vines. Nick lay sideways, propped on one elbow and Jessie sat with her legs curled up underneath her. She plucked at blades of grass as she spoke. "Okay, to understand this next bit you have to know something about me." She hesitated. "I just don't want...just don't..."

"What?"

"Just don't get all sentimental about it, okay?"

Nick nodded warily. "Okay."

Jessie took a breath, then spoke in a practiced monotone. "My parents died in a car crash when I was fifteen years old. One weekend they decided to take a trip to Cedar Rapids and I wanted to stay at home because my friend was having a birthday party and I didn't want to miss it. So, they left and they never came back. I went to live with my grandparents and when I was eighteen they agreed to let me move back into my parents' old house, where I've lived ever since. Yes, it was very sad, but I'm okay. I've learned to live with it."

She took another breath to continue her story but Nick cut in.

"What were their names?"

Jessie looked up, meeting his eyes. She was surprised by the question. "What?"

"Your parents. What were their names?"

Jessie smiled instinctively. "Jim. And Bonnie."

She stretched out and rolled onto her stomach, propping herself up on her elbows. "This is where it starts to get a bit weird," she warned. She was surprised that she was actually going to tell him this. That she was going to tell anyone.

"When I say that I've lived in the same town for fifteen years, that's exactly what I mean. Literally."

She glanced at Nick and she could see by his bland expression that he didn't get it.

"I've never been outside the town," she expanded. She leaned towards him, holding his eyes. "Ever."

She could see the comprehension dawning slowly and she pressed home her point. "Not for a holiday, not for a weekend trip or even a day trip, not to visit friends or relatives, not to go to weddings or funerals."

Nick asked the question she expected.

"Why?"

Jessie looked down at the grass patch in front of her, a little depleted after her nervous plucking.

"I was scared," she said plainly. "After what happened to my parents, from then on, that's what leaving town meant to me."

Nick looked confused. "Didn't your grandparents try to get you help? If it's like a phobia—"

Jessie shook her head, trying to explain. "It was never really an issue. We never went anywhere and I didn't really know I was avoiding it. I didn't want to go to college, I wanted to be a librarian like my grandmother. By the time I realized what I was doing it had become an ingrained habit and it never really seemed a big enough thing to actually get help for. So I never went anywhere, so what? I was happy with my life, I have my job, my friends, my dog. And there was always a feasible excuse if someone wanted me to go somewhere. I had to work, I couldn't leave Toby..." Jessie shrugged.

"Until you won this competition," said Nick.

"Exactly."

"So you decided that this was your big chance, that you were going to take the leap?"

"Well, I didn't so much decide as have it decided for me. There was just no excuse good enough to get me out of it. Everyone knew about it, everyone knew how much I liked your show." She grinned impulsively. "Everyone was teasing me about spending ten days on a tropical paradise island with Nick Garrett, sex god."

Nick winced. "Hey!"

She shrugged. "It's not my fault that you've got that reputation."

"But I haven't," he protested indignantly. "I mean, that's just an angle the tabloids like to play up sometimes, but it's got nothing to do with the real me."

"Oh, you poor misunderstood sex god," she teased.

"Weren't we talking about you?" Nick said archly.

Jessie went on, increasingly happy that he wasn't treating her like a crazy person after what she'd just told him. "That's it, basically. As crazy as it is, the first trip I ever take out of town and I put myself straight into a survival situation. I mean, I'm being attacked by sharks for crying out loud!"

Nick laughed. "So, how do you like it?"

"This week has been so incredible," she said simply. "There's a whole big world out there and I'm capable of being out in it. I'm learning that I can look after myself and I don't need to be protected from life."

"You're saying I should have let the shark get you?" Nick teased.

She pushed his shoulder playfully. "No. Believe me, I'm very grateful you were there."

"Me, too," he said. "And I actually like the fact that you're strong and determined." His mouth curled into a smile. "I like the way you jump into things and keep your sense of humor, especially when things are going wrong. I like that you're smart and funny and the farthest thing from a damsel-in-distress that I could possibly imagine." He paused. "That's why I keep wanting to kiss you."

Jessie met his eyes and he didn't look away, just held her gaze steadily. She moved forward and Nick moved the rest of the way until their mouths met in a kiss that started out as tender but quickly grew more insistent. Jessie opened her mouth as she felt his tongue pushing at her and her heart started to beat rapidly as she felt the hunger in his kiss. She let out a small moan and they closed the gap between them, bodies reaching for each other. Jessie sighed again as she felt his arms close around her, pulling her tight against him. She arched her body into his, thrilling to the pressure of his hard chest against her breasts. One of his legs moved between hers and she pressed her thighs against it, moving sensuously as she explored his mouth with her tongue. Heat spread through her as she felt him groan and she pushed her fingers through his hair, reveling in the strong effect she was having on him.

His hands moved searchingly over her, caressing her lower back, then stroking upwards over her shoulder blades before sweeping down again to grasp her thigh.

His shirt quickly became an obstacle and she fumbled at the buttons before pushing it upwards on his chest. He pulled his shirt and T-shirt off together and then looked at her, his breathing heavy. Jessie rose to her knees in front of him and he copied her, staring at her with dark eyes, full of desire. He played his hand across her collarbone and Jessie caught her bottom lip between her teeth, feeling an insistent pulse between her legs. She swayed towards him but he just smiled, kissing her with a tantalizing gentleness, flicking his tongue teasingly against her lips. He put his hands on her waist and his fingers moved downwards over her thighs as she sighed and pushed her tongue into his mouth, desperate to taste and feel him. She felt him lifting her dress and she raised her arms as he pulled it off gently.

Her body throbbed again as she watched him looking at her. He ran his fingers along the top of her strapless bra and she could feel her nipples straining against the lace. Then he lowered his head to the rise of her breasts, tasting and teasing with his tongue as Jessie closed her eyes and breathed in sharply. His hands caressed the bare skin of her waist as he kissed her slowly, up and down along her neck and shoulders until she was trembling. She reached for him, but he opened her bra and pushed her back, lowering his head to her nipples which were hard and aching.

Jessie cried out as his tongue circled the tight buds, first one and then the other and she pulled his head tight against her, her body straining for release. Nick lowered her to the ground gently. His mouth found hers again as his hand moved down her stomach and onto her panties. His fingers found the wetness immediately and Jessie gasped as a hot jolt of desire coursed through her. Nick moved his fingers firmly against her and she pressed her mouth against his shoulder, tasting salt as her breathing became more and more ragged. She rocked her hips against him and cried out as the pressure built. His fingers slipped inside her panties and he stroked her until she bucked and cried out as the tension exploded inside her.

Nick held her as her tremors faded and then her mouth searched for his again. Her hands reached for his waistband and he helped her take off his trousers, smiling at her as he slipped her panties off.

Jessie looked at him, breathless with desire and wonder at the sight of his hard, toned body. She reached down and held him, stroking tenderly at first and then tightening her grip as his breathing caught. He put his hand on the nape of her neck and drew her towards him again, plundering her mouth with his tongue.

Their mouths moved hungrily over each other and Nick pulled her up so that she was astride him, his hands cupping her thighs. Jessie was trembling and burning with the need to have him inside her.

She reached over and emptied her purse roughly, pulling out the condoms. Nick put one on and then put his hands on her bottom, guiding her.

She stared into his eyes as she pushed herself all the way onto him, gasping as she felt him fill her up.

She moved slowly, relishing the feel of him, unable to focus on anything except the incredible powerful heat building between her legs as she rocked, drawing him in further each time. Heat spread like wildfire through her veins and she splayed her hands on his chest, breathing hard. Her body began to move of its own accord and Jessie gave herself over to the relentless urge as she drove herself onto him again and again.

Nick groaned as he clutched at her thighs and as Jessie's thrusting grew more urgent he sat up and held her tightly, his face buried in her shoulder as he cried out with the climax that surged through them.

They breathed together in gasps, half-laughing as their racing hearts slowed. Nick played his tongue along her lips as Jessie stroked his face and twined her fingers in his hair. They lay down and Nick put his arm under her neck as Jessie rested her head on his chest, feeling his heart beating strongly.

She gazed at the hibiscus plants and the tahinu bushes, not really seeing any of it. She had never made love outside before, she'd never really made love like that before at all. She hadn't been aware of anything except Nick. Both her body and mind had been completely focused and wrapped in him.

She moved her hand, running her fingers over the parallel scars on his side.

"Leopard," she murmured.

"You weren't so bad yourself, tiger," he answered.

Jessie propped herself onto her elbow, looking down into his eyes as she laughed. He lifted his head and kissed her, catching her lip gently between his, before lying back down again, watching her with an affectionate expression that made warmth rush through her again.

She looked away, slightly frightened by the intensity of her desire. He reached up to brush a strand of hair back from her face and she spotted another scar.

"What's that?" she said.

He tilted his arm, checking. "A fall from a horse. His hoof caught me." Nick chuckled. "I was making a program about a dude ranch in Texas."

"I remember that show," she laughed, touching the scar tenderly. "It made me want to go there."

"Now you can," he murmured, running the back of his hand softly along her arm.

She looked down at him again, smiling. "We are near the Horse Latitudes, so that's a start." She frowned. "Oh, wait, they're in the Atlantic."

"How on earth do you know that?" he asked in amusement.

Jessie shrugged. "I like to read," she said simply. "Some things stick in the memory."

"Is that why you became a librarian?" he asked. "So you could just sit around reading all day?"

She responded to his teasing with a grin. "Pretty much. I figured that that and my natural nosiness would make me perfect for the job."

"Nosiness?" he asked. "Where does that come into it?"

She stroked her hand absently along his stomach. "You find out so much as a librarian," she said eagerly. "People come along looking for the oddest things. Sometimes they're taking up a new hobby or they want to find a particular poem that someone told them about. Or they're tracing their ancestry or want to find an inspiring biography. Sometimes they want information on a specific illness or disease." Her voice dropped an octave. "That always makes me a bit sad." She brightened up again. "But then I feel good about being able to help. And then there's the regulars. People who go through a book a day! Everyone's got their preferences. Thrillers, romances, the latest John Grisham, you name it. And there are the retirees who come in every day to read the papers and have a bit of a chat." She giggled. "There's a guy who comes in once a week and he's been researching his thesis for years! It's on some obscure sixteenth century poet who wrote, I think, one and a half poems. And there's a girl who's grimly determined to read all the classics. Jane Austen, Dickens, Faulkner, that sort of thing. Every month without fail. You have to admire her tenacity." Jessie suddenly stopped short, aware that she'd been rambling.

Nick didn't seem to mind. He was watching her through half-closed eyes, running a strand of her hair through his fingers.

She smiled at him, feeling relaxed and comfortable and then she tilted his arm to check his watch.

She crinkled her nose. "We should probably think about getting back—before we're missed and people start putting two and two together."

He continued to stroke her hair. "So you're not going to go back and tell all this to the confession cam?"

Jessie laughed and then she looked at him worriedly. "You don't really think I'd do that, do you?"

He shrugged. "How do I know you didn't do this to get ahead in the ratings?"

Jessie frowned. "Stop it, that's not funny." She drew back. "You don't really think I'm the kind of person who would—"

He drew her back into his arms, cutting off her indignant protestations with a long, slow kiss. Jessie sank against him, sliding her arms around to hold him as she kissed him back.

Nick pulled away eventually, looking into her eyes. "So we're not going to tell anyone about this?"

"I don't want to," said Jessie honestly. "I don't want Lois

turning it into a selling point or people putting up their comments on the Web site." She shivered in repulsion at the idea.

Nick touched her lips and cheeks with butterfly kisses. "Deal," he said. "It's just between you and me." He pulled his arm gently from under her neck. "I'll go first. You can lie here for a while and get your strength back."

Jessie smiled, letting her fingers trail down the muscles of his back as he stood up and started to dress. She lay on the grass, amazed and delighted that she didn't feel any shyness under his admiring gaze and then he gave her a last look and was gone.

Jessie closed her eyes, savoring the warmth of the sun on her skin and drifting in and out of sleep as she replayed the afternoon in her mind.

CINDI WAS ONCE AGAIN acting out a scene, but to Jessie's relief, she'd picked Malcolm as her victim this time. He was thrilled.

Jessie was sitting under a coconut tree, fanning herself with a palm leaf as she dozed and half-listened to them. As far as she could make out, it was some sort of "jealous mistress" scene. Malcolm was the married man and Cindi was playing the woman that he was trying to dump.

Cindi was shaking her head in bewilderment as Malcolm stood with his hands folded, doing a good impression of a very uncomfortable man.

"I don't understand," said Cindi. "What do you mean, 'slow down a little'?"

"Look, we both knew that this day would come," said Malcolm.

Jessie snuck a peek at Nick, allowing her eyes to linger for less than a second. Any longer than that and she was afraid she'd betray herself. She felt a frisson of excitement run through her again and she closed her eyes, trying desperately not to smile. Closing her eyes only made it all the more easy to conjure up the image of her and Nick, bodies entwined as they made love. Jessie's skin tingled and she opened her eyes again, trying to keep her breathing steady.

She'd been surprised that she'd reached the camp before him but the reason for his delay had immediately been apparent when he'd arrived an hour later and he did promise that the dead pig slung over his shoulder wasn't the one that Jessie had the bizarre love/hate relationship with.

The one quick moment of eye contact that she'd shared with Nick had been enough to have the blood rushing to Jessie's face so she'd stayed sitting safely under her tree after that.

She snuck another peek at him. He had hung the carcass from a strong branch to drain the blood and he was busy digging a roasting pit. He was doing an impressive job of pretending that nothing had happened. Jessie watched from under her eyelashes as he got up and went over to check on the pig.

Malcolm looked over. "Is it ready?"

Nick shook his head and Cindi snapped her fingers crossly in Malcolm's face. "Focus!"

"Sorry," he said meekly. "Where were we?"

"Okay, this is where I start to get an edge of desperation and you're becoming more and more removed. You're also dealing with feelings of guilt because you know that you used me, so you're trying to convince both me *and* yourself that you never made any promises. Remember what I said about putting 'layers' into your performance?"

Malcolm nodded, eager as a puppy. "This is so great."

Jessie smiled as she watched him get-into-character.

He cleared his throat. "Look," he said pleadingly. "I always told you that I loved my wife and I wasn't going to leave her. What we had was wonderful, but I think it's time to stop." He put out one hand and stroked Cindi's arm. "Before one of us really gets hurt."

Cindi leaned towards him. "What if I don't want to stop?" she said plaintively.

Malcolm took back his hand, chewing at his lip. "I think we should," he said definitively.

"But...but you said you loved me." Cindi looked distraught.

Malcolm looked at the ground. "And in a way, I did."

Ouch, thought Jessie. Malcolm was better at this than she would have expected. Maybe all men had this speech hardwired into their brains at birth. The thought made her smile.

"So that's all I was to you?" said Cindi bitterly. "Just a bit of fun?"

"We both agreed that it wasn't going to be anything permanent."

"And you think you can just throw me aside now. Now that you're tired of me?"

Malcolm shook his head sadly. "We both went into this with our eyes wide open. Don't pretend that you didn't know this day would come."

Jessie's smile faded a little. The scene was beginning to graze a bit too close to the bone for her liking. She took a quick look at Nick to see if he'd noticed.

If it was bothering him he gave no sign of it. In fact, he seemed completely unperturbed, both by the scene and Jessie's presence.

A tiny churlish voice popped into her head. *Gosh, it must be easy to be a man. Have sex, kill a pig, make a fire, dig a pit...all in a day's work.*

She frowned. Wasn't he just doing exactly what they'd agreed to do? Pretend nothing had happened?

Her mind started to poke at the thought. They'd both said that they should keep it hidden from the cameras but, now that Jessie thought about it, what was the reason? Would it really be so awful if it came out?

Okay, they didn't have to admit to having sex, but surely it would be no big deal to admit that there was *something* going on.

Cindi's voice interrupted her perusals. "Okay, Kenny, this is where you start to come in for the close-ups. I'm going for a lot of different emotions here. I'm upset but also angry." She winked at Malcolm. "Remember what I said about 'layers'? And I'm also feeling foolish because of course I knew deep down that he'd never leave his wife."

At least I didn't have an affair with a married man, Jessie told herself encouragingly. I'm not that dumb.

Her inner voice laughed merrily and launched into a diatribe. Excuse me? Aren't you? You mean you haven't been wondering what's going to happen next with you and Nick? Whether you're going to have another lagoon encounter or if you're going to wait until after the show to meet in private. I mean, did he mention anything about meeting after the show? I don't think he did. Did I miss it?

Boy, thought Jessie, when did my inner voice become so sarcastic?

She closed her eyes again, telling herself not to get so worked up. The sex had been great and she didn't regret it and she wasn't going to ruin the memory by tying herself in knots over it.

She still had that, didn't she? The great memory of it?

Jessie opened her eyes.

Now that she thought about it, how come he *hadn't* said anything about meeting up after the show?

She looked across the beach, relieved to see Lois's motorboat pulling up onto the shore. Lois might be a pain but at least she was a distracting pain.

"Great," said Lois, trotting up towards them. "I'm glad

you're all here." She stopped by Nick and looked down at him, putting her hands on her hips. "Nick, we lost you off camera while you were tracking the pig. We didn't get the kill."

Nick waited, then looked dubiously at the carcass. "It's not like I can do it again."

Lois sighed. "Funny. I'm just saying, next time, could you please have Kenny with you? There are other pigs, right?"

"I'll do my best, Lois."

She narrowed her eyes but then got distracted by the others.

"Jessie, I wanted to talk to you. About you and Nick."

Jessie's mouth went dry. "About us?"

Lois nodded. "Yeah. About the two of you having sex."

8

"I CAN'T BELIEVE YOU TOLD—"

"Eighty-four percent think it's a good—"

Jessie and Lois broke off at the same time and stared at each other.

"What?" said Jessie, sweat prickling her armpits.

Lois dipped her head and peered over the top of her sunglasses. "What were you going to say?"

Jessie could feel the tension radiating off Nick. "Nothing," she croaked. "You go ahead."

Lois stared hard at her for a moment, then looked down at her clipboard. "Eighty-four percent of our audience think it's a good idea," she repeated.

"What is?" asked Nick cautiously.

"For you and Jessie to hook up. They think you'd make a cute couple."

Jessie didn't know what to say. She tried an incredulous laugh but it came out sounding forced and hollow.

"What?" yelled Cindi. "How come Jessie gets him? Why doesn't anyone want me to have him?"

Jessie wanted to hug Cindi for reminding her what a natural reaction sounded like.

"Uh-uh," she teased Cindi. "He's all mine."

Lois flipped through her notes. "Cindi, everyone thinks Malcolm's cheating on his wife with you. That's why it's only fair that Jessie gets Nick."

"That's ridiculous," said Malcolm hotly. "There's nothing

going on with me and Cindi." He frowned. "Is it because of that scene we were doing? That was just acting. Cindi isn't my mistress. I mean, I don't have a mistress."

Lois looked pleased. "I haven't seen that yet. That sounds interesting."

Malcolm chewed at his lip. "You'll have to be careful when you broadcast it, so that you don't give the wrong impression."

Lois scribbled a note to herself. "I *will* have to be careful of that," she murmured.

Jessie was glad that the attention had shifted from herself and Nick but she felt sorry for Malcolm who was looking rather ashen.

"Anyway," said Lois brightly. "As you can see, our audience are all dying to hear if there's any romance or well, anything at all going on. I know I talked to each of you about it before and I think it was Jess who was complaining that all the survival chores and challenges don't leave you with much time or energy for romance."

Jessie's mouth fell open. "I wasn't complaining," she denied strongly. "It was an *explanation!*"

Lois dismissed her with a casual wave of her hand. "Sure, sure. The point is, we've decided to grease the wheels." She made a face. "I'll be honest with you. Even if we don't have sex on the show we do need the *promise* of it if we're going to keep the audience interest. So, we're going to install a hot tub." She put up her hand as Nick started to protest. "Look, Nick, given a few weeks or months I'm sure you could build a hot tub out of some twigs and tree bark so let's just assume that you did, okay?"

"Oh, please let her," begged Cindi. "I'd give my left leg to get into a hot tub right now."

Nick folded his arms, an unhappy scowl on his face.

"And we'll have a crate of wine 'wash up' on the shore,"

continued Lois, ignoring his displeasure. "You guys can make a night of it."

Nick snorted.

Jessie was made slightly nervous by the prospect of a drunken hot tub night but, wanting to blend in, she put on a happy face like the others.

"Just enjoy it," said Lois. "See where the night takes you. Don't be afraid to get down and dirty, either. You're all adults."

Jessie attempted to be the voice of reason. "Well, we can't exactly have sex on camera," she said.

"Don't be so defeatist," Lois scoffed. "There are plenty of bushes, aren't there? And you have your shelters. Look at teenagers, for goodness' sakes. They're under the watchful eyes of their parents and you always hear about them sneaking off to have sex."

Jessie didn't follow the logic. "We're not teenagers."

"Exactly," said Lois triumphantly. "You're consenting adults and so even more resourceful. So, don't be afraid to go wild, we can always edit it out."

JESSIE COULD FEEL Cindi's eyes boring into her.

She concentrated on gathering the arrowroot plants.

"So," said Cindi conversationally. "How was it?"

Jessie looked up. "How was what?"

Cindi smiled. "The sex. With Nick."

"What are you talking about?" said Jessie, creasing her brow in bemusement.

"Oh, don't play dumb with me." Cindi put on a singsong voice. "You slept with Ni-ick."

Jessie knew that she was lucky that Kenny had stayed with the men. She was sure that the handheld camera would have caught the nervousness in her eyes but she felt that, given the distance, she could fool both the Island Eyes and Cindi. She had to.

She let her mouth open in a surprised gasp. "Excuse me?" she said in amusement.

"You slept with Nick," said Cindi. "And what I want to know is where and how? And, of course, how was it? Fantastic, right?"

Jessie laughed again. "Are you crazy?"

"Oh, give it up," complained Cindi. "I heard you. When Lois was talking about you and Nick, you looked at him and said 'I can't believe you told her.' Lois didn't hear it because she was talking, but I heard it. So, come on, I want details."

Jessie furrowed her brow as if thinking back and then she smiled widely.

"Oh, okay," she said patronizingly. "I see what you mean. No, I'd thought that maybe he told Lois we'd slept together, to boost the ratings or something. So what I was going to say was, *I can't believe you told her we slept together when that's completely untrue.*" Jessie laughed again, ducking down to brush some sand from the graze on her leg.

She straightened up. Cindi was still watching her suspiciously.

"Really? There's nothing going on?"

Jessie laughed heartily. "Me and Nick? God, no." She pressed forward a new subject. "It's pretty funny what she said about you and Malcolm, too, isn't it? Boy, she's sure got some crazy ideas. Sex on the brain."

Protesting too much, her inner voice warned her.

"I don't care what her reasons are," said Cindi, grinning. "I'm just looking forward to tonight. Hot tub, a few glasses of wine, it'll be heaven."

"Mmm," said Jessie, trying to fake some enthusiasm.

"You might get a chance with Nick after all," teased Cindi.

"Yeah, right," scoffed Jessie.

"You're not interested?" asked Cindi in disbelief.

"Haven't you forgotten something," Jessie pointed out. "We're surrounded by cameras."

Cindi lifted her eyebrows suggestively. "But if there were no cameras, you'd go for it, right?"

Jessie pursed her lips. "I don't know, Cindi. I mean, we just met, I hardly know him." She knew she was sounding like the epitome of the prudish librarian but it was in a good cause.

"So what?" said Cindi. "It's Nick Garrett!" She started to pull the heads off the plants they'd collected, stacking the tubers in a neat pile. "I totally would."

"Would what?" asked Jessie warily.

"Whatever," said Cindi salaciously. "He's gorgeous."

Jessie felt cold. She attempted a bantering tone. "You haven't done anything so far, have you?"

"No," said Cindi.

Jessie breathed a silent sigh of relief.

Cindi giggled. "But we'll see how tonight goes."

NICK PAUSED AS MALCOLM stood up and looked out towards the ocean again.

"You really don't have to help," he said.

"I want to," said Malcolm, taking a few deep breaths. "It just takes some getting used to, that's all."

"You're going great," said Nick. He looked over at Kenny who was eating an apple as he filmed, a picture of indifference. "Despite appearances, it took Kenny some time to get used to the gory stuff as well."

Nick went back to skinning the pig and speaking to the camera. "I try not to cut the skin as I'm taking it off because it'll make for a bigger piece of leather when we dry it out. Very useful for shoes and clothes."

Malcolm, still looking out at the waves, spoke hesitantly, the worry evident in his voice.

"You don't think Lois will put anything on the program about me and Cindi, do you?"

Nick looked up. "There's nothing going on is there?"

Malcolm looked around, aghast. "No, of course not! I'm a married man. Happily married."

"Then I'm sure it'll be fine."

Malcolm didn't look reassured. "I'm just worried that Lois might twist things. You know, for the sake of the show. But she wouldn't do that, would she? Just to boost the ratings?"

Nick didn't want to say anything that would make Malcolm feel worse, but Kenny let out a snort. Malcolm looked at him, then back at Nick. "Would she?"

Nick shrugged apologetically. "Lois really loves her job."

"But I love my wife!"

Nick nodded. "I'm sure you do. And I'm sure she knows that. Don't worry, it'll be fine."

Malcolm turned towards the trees, looking randomly for cameras. "I miss you, honey!" he yelled. "I really do."

Cindi and Jessie looked at each other in confusion, then shrugged and waved at him.

Malcolm slapped his forehead. "Great," he said, sitting down beside Nick again. "Now you can come to my house after the show and watch my wife skin *me* alive."

"Don't worry," said Nick, laughing kindly. "I'm sure she's very proud of you."

"There's nothing going on," said Malcolm again.

"Of course not," repeated Nick.

"Like there's nothing going on with you and Jessie," said Malcolm.

Nick cut away some more of the skin, pretending to be distracted. He hadn't been able to stop thinking about the sex with Jessie. It had been amazing but what he'd liked even more was the way they'd talked and laughed, as if they'd known each other for a long time. That had been a close call moment with Lois and he could still picture the pulse beating in Jessie's neck when she thought she'd let the cat out of the bag. He hoped that all this talk of audience interest wouldn't make her regret what had happened between them.

"Of course there's nothing going on with Jessie and me," said Nick, fighting the smile that wanted to spread across his face. "I'm just here to make a show."

"And I'm happily married," said Malcolm.

"Okay then."

"Okay."

JESSIE WAS DRINKING very slowly, barely sipping her wine. She had noticed that Nick wasn't drinking at all. He was pretending to but the level in his glass never went down, except when he went to check the fire or the generator for the hot tub and then he always came back with an empty glass.

Malcolm and Cindi were making up for Jessie and Nick however. Even the huge dinner of leftover roast pig that they'd had didn't seem to be doing much to soak up the alcohol in their case. Kenny had gone back to the yacht, presumably in the hopes that without the camera in their faces they would be more inclined to give Lois what she was looking for.

The hot tub was big enough that they could all sit without touching each other, to Jessie's profound relief. Malcolm had been very uptight for the first hour, apologizing profusely if his toe nudged up against someone's leg and Jessie hadn't blamed him. They'd all felt a bit awkward at first but after a while it was impossible not to succumb to the warm bubbles massaging them and the wine seeping into their bloodstreams. They'd relaxed and stopped apologizing because, after all, it was only feet and calves.

And muscular shoulders and glistening chests. Okay, that was just Nick but Jessie had to keep reminding herself not to stare. It was just that Nick's body was no longer just a body. The chest hairs, the scar on his elbow, the strong muscles in his legs—Jessie could still feel all of it in her fingertips. And her own body was tingling and glowing, too, just from his proximity.

She was a little annoyed because they'd all started off by sitting equidistant from each other, around the edge of the tub but Cindi had gradually edged over until she was next to Nick and Malcolm had somehow drifted sideways until he was next to Jessie.

They were effectively split into two couples. Unfortunately for Jessie, the wrong two. After what Cindi had said earlier, Jessie wasn't crazy about having her cozied up to Nick, especially when Nick didn't seem to be backing away. She told herself that Nick was probably just being friendly to Cindi to draw attention away from himself and Jessie.

And in that way, the setup wasn't too bad. If Jessie was sitting next to him she'd have been much too self-conscious to talk to him. This way they could carry on a flirtation without anyone realizing it. Their eyes met occasionally and each time Jessie felt a hot frisson of excitement run through her.

Cindi was holding forth on the subject of sex. They had all started out chatting about life on the island but as the drink took effect it seemed to make the others tired and Cindi aggressive. They were content to let her monopolize the conversation with her rambling and disjointed thoughts.

"...and on some islands there's no such thing as marriage. People just have sex with whoever they want and kids are raised in a community setting." She squinted thoughtfully.

"And what's the name of those women that had their own tribe?"

"Amazons," supplied Jessie.

"That's it! Amazons. They could pick and choose."

"Actually, there were no men in the Amazon race," said Jessie. "They had sex with men in neighboring tribes and any sons that were born were killed or sent back to their fathers."

"There are no men in Manhattan, either," grumbled Cindi. "None worth having, that is. They're all crazy, especially in the movie business. You must know what I mean, Nick."

His eyebrows dipped downwards. "I don't really think of myself as being in the movie business."

"Movies, TV, whatever. Everyone has an agenda," Cindi rambled on. "Guys might seem perfectly great in the beginning but then they turn out to be passive-aggressive narcissists when you get to know them. Or just plain weird."

"I'm glad I'm married," Malcolm said as Cindi paused to drink. "I remember the first time I saw Debbie. It was at my cousin's wedding and I hadn't even really wanted to go, but my sister said I had to. Debbie was a bridesmaid and she was so beautiful."

Cindi peered at him. "You saw her in a bridesmaid's dress and you thought she was beautiful?"

Malcolm nodded.

"Wow," said Cindi. "That's love."

"I think it's good luck to meet your spouse at a wedding," said Malcolm. "It sure was for us."

"What's that saying?" said Cindi, frowning in thought. "Marriage is the price that men pay for sex and sex is the price women pay for marriage."

"That's stupid," said Jessie impulsively. "Women enjoy sex just as much as men. When it's done right."

All three heads turned to look at her and she blushed brick red.

"I think it's so cute that you blush whenever you talk about sex," said Cindi. "It's such a 'librarian' thing to do."

Nick looked at her, his eyes sparkling with amusement. "Yeah, it's cute."

"And of course women enjoy sex," Cindi went on. "I'm just saying that it's also a currency." She waved her wine-glass for emphasis. "You'd be amazed how many women will sleep with someone just to get a part. Well, you mightn't be amazed, Nick. I'm sure you've had plenty of experience of it."

Jessie looked hurriedly at Nick.

He seemed confused. "What do you mean?"

Cindi put her hand to her mouth and widened her eyes. "Ooh, I didn't mean personal experience. I'm not implying that you've done it." Cindi scrunched up her nose as she tried to make herself understood. "I'm sure you haven't slept with women just because they wanted to be on your show— I'm just saying you must have had offers."

Jessie felt a pang of disquiet as Nick's expression flickered. "Not really," he said, not looking over at her.

Jessie took a sip of wine, wondering how many women exactly "not really" added up to.

Cindi frowned and then her face cleared. "You're right, what woman in her right mind would actually *want* to be on this show?" She patted Nick's arm. "They probably just wanted to sleep with you."

Jessie spluttered as her wine went down the wrong way. She seriously considered grabbing Cindi's ankle and pulling her under the water, anything to shut her up.

"You okay?" said Nick, grinning knowingly at Jessie.

Jessie nodded, thumping her chest as her eyes watered. "I'm fine."

"Hey, you know what would be fun?" said Cindi.

Jessie's heart sank. As she'd watched glass after glass of wine disappear down Cindi's throat she knew it was only a matter of time before she decided to go topless.

Well, she'd be doing it on her own.

"Doing the confession cam," said Cindi. "I've got some things I'd like to say to a few people."

They all looked at each other dubiously.

"That's probably not such a good idea," said Jessie.

Cindi swirled the wine in her glass, still considering it.

Malcolm sighed heavily. "I should do the confession cam. I want to tell Debbie how much I miss her. How much I love her."

Cindi opened her mouth to speak, but Malcolm wasn't finished. "I love her," he said fervently. "I really do. She's wonderful."

"Of course she is," said Jessie. She looked over and caught Nick's gaze. She was struggling to hold in her laughter and one glance told her he was having the same problem.

"The thing is," said Malcolm, gesturing as if he was about to reveal a profound truth, "that she fell in love with me even though I was just an ordinary guy, and kinda tubby." He gestured down at his body. "Now I've lost weight and I've got a tan."

They all looked at him while he took a sip of wine. He covered his mouth and burped conclusively.

Jessie and Nick locked eyes again and Jessie couldn't help letting out a short burst of laughter. She disguised it as a cough.

Cindi finished off her wine with a gulp and giggled as she turned around in the water.

"Oops, sorry, Nick," she said, falling against him.

She rose unsteadily to her feet and leaned out over the edge of the tub, her pert bottom nudging Nick's shoulder as she poured the last of the bottle into her glass. Jessie looked away, trying to ignore the knot of jealous possessiveness in her stomach.

Malcolm's mouth was hanging open and Jessie put her fingers under his chin, closing it so sharply that his teeth clicked.

Nick let out a burst of laughter and Cindi turned.

"What? What did I miss?"

"Nothing," said Nick, grinning at Jessie. She smiled happily, not the slightest bit intimidated by the narrow-eyed look from Cindi.

Cindi slid back into the water. "Oooh," she said, stretching. "I'm so warm and tingly." She smiled up at Nick.

"Anybody want to hear about tomorrow's challenge?" he said, ignoring her.

"Can't we just forget about all that stuff for one night?" complained Cindi. "Please, Nick. Come on, relax and enjoy yourself."

"I am enjoying myself," he said, holding Jessie's gaze. She gave him a secretive smile. She had a tiny niggling worry that maybe he was referring to the fact that Cindi was draped all over him, but she shook it off.

Cindi struggled to her feet and they all lifted their glasses out of the way of the ensuing tidal wave.

"Excuse me for a moment," said Cindi. "I have to go to the little girl's room." She tapped Nick on the shoulder. "Don't you go anywhere."

She giggled helplessly as she climbed out of the hot tub and descended the steps.

"Did she finish that bottle?" said Malcolm, causing another tsunami as he stood up and leaned over the edge of the tub, searching for more wine.

Jessie and Nick looked at each other and then looked away, each smiling. It seemed to Jessie that regardless of all the talking that had gone on all night the real conversation had been in her eye contact with Nick.

Or in the way his toe was nudging her thigh now.

She surreptitiously brushed it away.

"I think Cindi sometimes forgets she's *on camera*," she told him.

"You're right," said Nick blandly. He quirked an eyebrow. "Are you enjoying yourself?"

Jessie smiled widely. "Yes, this hot tub is fantastic."

"I'm glad to hear that."

Jessie was sure that there was a body-language expert somewhere right at that moment springing out of her armchair and exclaiming, "They *did* it!" She just hoped they were hiding it from everyone else.

"I guess I'd better find an easy challenge for tomorrow," said Nick. "I don't think anyone's going to be in great shape."

Jessie nodded and then put up her hand as a huge yawn got her.

"You must have used up a lot of energy today," said Nick.

Jessie smiled. "I did a lot of walking," she purred. "And, of course, there's the wine."

"Of course," he said, "that explains it."

They hoisted their glasses again as Malcolm turned and lowered himself into the water once more.

Jessie rose carefully to her feet. "I think I'll go and check on Cindi," she said. "Make sure she doesn't get lost this time."

"And you and I can talk, Nick," said Malcolm. "Man to man."

Jessie grinned as Nick gave her a pleading look.

"WE SHOULD COMPLAIN to the management," said Cindi, giggling as she emerged. "There are no mirrors in there." She stopped and swayed on her feet, fanning her face. "How do

I look? Am I flushed?" She leaned towards Jessie and then exploded with laughter, doubling over. "Did I say *flushed?* Oh, God, no pun intended."

Jessie watched her as she giggled maniacally and then straightened up, hiccupping as her laughter trailed off.

"Seriously though..." said Cindi, wiping tears from the corners of her eyes. "Do I look okay? Is my face red?"

Jessie reached out and made some pointless adjustments to Cindi's hair and she lifted the strap of her bra back onto her shoulder. In doing so she realized they'd left the microphones behind them by the hot tub.

Perfect.

She pointed it out to Cindi and asked her next question with a complicit smile.

"So, how are you getting on with Nick? Making any progress there?"

Cindi made a face and blew a resounding raspberry. Jessie leaned back, surreptitiously wiping spray from her cheek.

"Dead loss," said Cindi. "I'm beginning to think that Nick might be a man's man."

Handel's *Messiah* played in stereo in Jessie's head. She hadn't really had any doubts but it was nice to have confirmation.

"Never mind," she consoled. "The hot tub is really relaxing isn't it? My muscles feel great."

"No kidding," said Cindi, doing some neck rolls. Her head fell forward and she blinked as she examined her breasts.

Jessie said, "So, I'm just going to pop in here and then we'll go back."

"Wait," said Cindi, motioning Jessie towards her with her hand. "Come here."

"What?" said Jessie in an equally hushed tone.

"Okay," Cindi said, putting her hand on Jessie's shoulder.

"Nick might be a flop but that doesn't mean that the night has to be a total washout." She winked at Jessie, her eyes glittering with devilment.

Jessie drew back slightly. "Uh, look, Cindi..."

Cindi swayed forward, following Jessie's motion. "I think Malcolm is missing wifey, if you know what I mean."

Jessie felt a burst of relief, then her brain processed what Cindi had said. "Wait a minute, you don't mean...?"

Cindi nodded.

"You wouldn't," said Jessie.

Cindi shrugged. "Hey, I'm surprised, too. But our Malcolm has toned up a bit in the last few days. It might be fun."

"But he's married," said Jessie. "Cindi, you can't."

Cindi thought for a moment, her eyes wandering. "That would mean that *he'd* be cheating, not me. It's not a problem for me."

"Not a problem?" said Jessie in disbelief. "Cindi, it would be on camera. His wife would see. The whole world would see."

"We could do it under a bush, like Lois said."

Jessie laughed at the absurdity. "I think people would figure it out. Cindi, his family would know. Your family! You've got to be joking me."

"What's the big deal?" retorted Cindi. "It would just be a bit of fun."

"Look, you're drunk. You don't really want to do this."

Cindi narrowed her eyes. "Maybe you just want him for yourself. Well, hands off, it was my idea first."

Jessie tried a different tack, appealing to Cindi's greed.

"Look," she said pragmatically, "if you do this the audience will hate you. You'll lose votes and you won't win the money. Come on, it's not worth losing a million bucks over him, is it?"

"Are you kidding me?" laughed Cindi. "Audiences love a bitch. It's *him* they won't vote for."

She turned towards the path back to the hot tub and Jessie grabbed her arm. "Cindi, wait." She struggled to find something else to dissuade Cindi, but then she slowly realized what was going on.

Jessie nodded, smiling in admiration. "Oh, I get it. This is one of your 'scenes,' isn't it?" Jessie shook her head in embarrassment. "I can't believe you got me again. Wow, you're good."

She let go of Cindi's arm. "I'm so dumb. I actually thought you were going to sleep with him."

Cindi folded her arms and bared her teeth in a feline smile. "I *am* going to sleep with him," she said. "And here's a 'scene' for you. You want to hear about audience votes, try this on for size. Audiences love a wronged woman even more than a bitch." Cindi's face changed, becoming plaintive. "I thought he was going to leave his wife." She unfolded her arms and pressed one hand to her chest, the personification of injured innocence. "He said he *loved* me."

Jessie felt a surge of anger. Cindi had crossed the line. She was messing with real people's lives and Jessie had to stop her. She had to get through to her somehow.

She stepped forward, using her height to loom threateningly over Cindi as she grabbed her arms.

"I'm warning you," she said, her eyes drilling into Cindi's. "You do this and you'll be in big trouble."

"Ow," whimpered Cindi. "You're hurting me."

"This is nothing. I'm going to be watching you like a hawk from now on and if you so much as give him a peck on the cheek you'll regret it. I mean it, Cindi, you keep away from him."

She thrust Cindi away from her and stormed off, back towards the hot tub, her skin crawling with disgust at the way she'd just behaved.

NICK STEPPED OUT of the trees, watching as Jessie strode away.

"What was that about?" he asked Cindi, stunned.

Cindi turned, putting her hand up to her mouth. "Nick? Did you hear it all?" she asked, her eyes wide.

"I just got here," he said. "I just caught the end." He looked towards the path where Jessie had disappeared. "Why was she so angry?"

Cindi didn't answer and he turned back in time to see her eyes fill with tears.

"It was awful," she said, a sob hiccupping in her throat. The tears overflowed and spilled down her cheeks. "I was just telling her how much I admired you and that I really liked you, as a friend, and she just went nuts." Cindi rubbed at her arms. "She was shaking me and telling me to keep away from you. I couldn't believe it."

Neither could Nick. He was appalled. If he hadn't seen it for himself he would never have believed Jessie was capable of such a jealous rage.

"I'm so glad you came along," said Cindi. She shivered, stepping towards him. "I thought she was going to hit me."

Nick hesitated and then let her huddle against him. He put his arms around her. "It's okay," he said. "It must have been some kind of misunderstanding."

Cindi clung to him and he stroked her hair, all of his thoughts on Jessie. He couldn't understand how he had misread her. He would have to say something to her.

Cindi pulled her head back from his chest and looked up at him, her eyes slightly unfocused.

"I'm so glad you came along, Nick," she said. He could feel her arching her body into his and one of her hands moved down his back and slipped under the waistband of his trousers. Great, this was all he needed.

"Your system isn't used to alcohol," he told Cindi as he

gently extricated himself from her grasp. "This is probably hitting you a lot harder than you're used to."

He turned her towards the path, one arm across her back to support her as she swayed.

"Come on," he said. "Let's get you to bed."

9

"COME ON, let's get you to bed."

Jessie put her hand over her mouth, not wanting to believe what she'd just seen. The film that Kenny was playing for her had been recorded by one of the hidden Island Eyes and it was grainy, but there was no mistaking the people in it. And since Nick had been wearing his microphone they had audio as well.

"It doesn't necessarily mean anything," said Kenny, switching off the video recorder.

"Hey, it doesn't make any difference to me," said Jessie. She shrugged and forced a laugh. "I think it's funny." She dipped her head as her bottom lip started trembling. "Let's face it, we all knew it was going to happen." She lifted her hand to look at her watch, then remembered that she wasn't wearing one, so she coughed instead.

"I'd better go and do the confession cam," she said to Kenny.

"Sure," he said. "See you later."

Jessie walked towards the tiki hut, trying to keep her breathing steady. She reached the hut but veered away, knowing that it was the last thing she could do right now.

"HOW DID SHE TAKE IT?" said Lois.

Kenny fiddled with the wide-angle lens setting. He'd trekked with Nick through humid jungles, he'd spent time getting slowly scorched in deserts and he'd gotten up close and personal with thundering bison, but this was the first time he'd ever really hated his job. He hadn't wanted to show the tape to Jessie at all, but Lois had insisted.

Well, Lois might have forced him into that, but Kenny had meant what he'd said to Nick. He did like Jessie. He found her genuine and kindhearted and he wasn't going to betray her to Lois. He wasn't going to mention the way her face had paled or the tremor in her voice.

"I don't think she cared at all," he said blandly. "She seemed to think it was funny."

Lois looked aggrieved. "Darn it," she said, shaking her head. "I would have sworn there was something going on with her and Nick." She exhaled, shrugging. "Oh, well, never mind. We're going to get a reaction out of her later on anyway, that's for sure."

THE RAFT THAT NICK had made was anchored a couple of hundred feet from shore where it made a perfect platform for taking a breather between swims or getting in some serious sunbathing.

Jessie had it to herself and she was lying facedown, wondering if she would ever be able to stop crying. She was hoping that the bobbing of the raft would disguise the heaving of her shoulders as another wave of sobs wracked her.

Nick and Cindi. It made her sick to her stomach to think of it.

After her showdown with Cindi the night before, Jessie had gone off to a secluded part of the forest for a while, just to calm down. The combination of the wine and the hot tub was a heady one and she'd felt much better after some fresh night air. She'd returned to the tub and found only Malcolm. He'd told her that Nick was gone to the tiki hut and, when Cindi didn't come back to the tub, Jessie assumed that she was so shaken she'd gone straight to bed.

After another ten minutes of listening to Malcolm droning on and on about how much he missed his wife, Jessie had retreated gratefully to the quietude of her own shelter. She'd even been feeling pleased with herself for saving Malcolm from Cindi's clutches. What an idiot. If only she'd left Cindi alone, the little blond vixen wouldn't have seduced Nick.

Oh, who was she fooling? It didn't matter what chain of events had led to it, the fact was that it had happened and it wasn't Cindi who was to blame, it was Nick.

How could she have been so wrong about him? How could she have been so foolish?

If it was just the tape evidence she would have automatically given him the benefit of the doubt and she would have found some way to explain it away.

But, soon after she'd gotten up that morning, Jessie had figured out that something was awry.

She had noticed immediately that Cindi, albeit hungover, had been smugly pleased with herself when she'd emerged from her shelter. Malcolm, on the other hand, had looked pale and sickly. Jessie had experienced a heart-sinking feeling, assuming that their respective demeanors had the same provenance, an injudicious romantic encounter.

Then Nick had returned to camp after a swim. Jessie had smiled hello and Nick had given her a very odd look before turning to Cindi to enquire about the severity of her hangover. Jessie had been taken aback, wondering if she'd unintentionally offended him by going to bed without saying good-night.

He'd continued to ignore her and she'd remained perplexed until Kenny had called her aside and supplied the missing piece of the puzzle.

She didn't know why Kenny had shown it to her but she suspected it was because he knew something about herself and Nick and was trying to protect her from really making a fool of herself. Then again, she could be way off the mark, ascribing him with such kindness. He was a man, too, wasn't he?

Jessie continued to weep, her whole body aching with anguish. Nick had just used her and she had no one to blame but herself. She had let him, encouraged him in fact. To think, she'd been entertaining fantasies about getting together with him after the show. She must have been out of her mind.

It looked like she'd been right about the real world after all. It was far too hurtful a place.

She wished she could stay floating on this raft forever. Just cut the rope and let herself drift out to sea.

She had no idea how she was supposed to get through the next four days.

JESSIE WAS ONLY ABLE to ignore Lois's frenetic waving for so long. When Lois started calling her name through a bullhorn Jessie surrendered and swam reluctantly back to shore.

She joined the group at camp and arranged her face into an indulgent expression as Lois teased them about what might have been caught on film the night before.

Nick looked unperturbed, but then, he would. He knew how to have sex without being caught on camera, didn't he?

During her deliberations on the raft, Jessie had managed to put aside her hurt and outrage long enough to decide on a plan of action; the only one really available to her. She was determined not to betray herself by any observable signs or emotional outbursts. She would just act as if nothing had happened. She realized now that she had no idea what Nick was capable of, but if he chose to bring it up, to expose her on camera, she'd be ready for him. She would just deny it completely.

She'd only met his eyes once, by accident and had been

unable to prevent her anger and hurt coming through in one quick glare.

Nick hadn't even flinched. Just looked away, shaking his head as if he was disappointed with her. The man had a heart of granite.

"Anyway," said Lois, cutting through her perusals, "you were all such good sports last night and all week that we've organized a little reward for you."

She beamed at them but Jessie knew that the others shared her reservations. Lois's idea of a reward wasn't necessarily everyone's.

Lois walked over and stood behind Malcolm, putting her hands on his shoulders. Kenny was nearby, recording the hunted look on Malcolm's face.

"Malcolm," said Lois. "Take a look down on shore. See who's been washed up from a serendipitous shipwreck?"

Malcolm followed her instructions with a fearful expression, almost as if he was expecting pirates but then his eyes filled with wonderment.

"Debbie?" he said, leaping to his feet. He winced and put a hand to his forehead, the hangover was obviously still there, as he stared down at the figure who was clambering gracelessly from a rowboat.

"Debbie!" he called, hurrying down towards her.

Lois snapped her fingers bossily at Kenny, motioning him to follow Malcolm and catch the joyous reunion between castaway man and wife.

"Aww, look at that," said Lois as the couple embraced. "So sweet." She turned to the others. "I bet you're all looking forward to getting some feedback from the real world about how the show is perceived." She caught her lip between her teeth in an attempt to convey edge-of-seat gripping excitement. "And see how you're all doing in the ratings."

Jessie was sorely tempted to roll her eyes so she looked

hurriedly away from Lois and in doing so, caught Nick watching her. He looked away but not before she registered his strange expression. Then, his face cleared and became welcoming as Malcolm and Debbie approached them.

Jessie squashed down the anger rising in her chest and joined the others in greeting Debbie.

Cindi caught Debbie's hands and drew her over to a log, introducing herself without any hesitation. "I'm Cindi, you have to tell me how I'm doing in the ratings. What are people saying about us?"

Even though she should have learned to expect it, Jessie was still nonplussed by Cindi's duplicity. Less than twelve hours before she'd been planning to seduce this woman's husband and now, here she was, acting like her best friend.

Debbie looked like she had in the photograph—shy, slightly dumpy and overawed, as if she wasn't used to anyone paying this much attention to her.

"It's all very exciting," she said in a soft mid-western accent. "Everyone talks about it in the supermarket and at church and such. I still can hardly believe that it's my Malcolm that's in it. It's like a dream." She looked shyly at Cindi. "Everyone really likes your 'acting' scenes—we all think you're so talented and funny."

Cindi clasped her hands to her chest. "I've died and gone to heaven. I don't care now if I win the money or not, that's all I need, that recognition."

Jessie could feel her eyeballs heading northward again, so she distracted herself.

"Hi, I'm Jessie," she said, holding out her hand to Debbie. "We've all heard so much about you and it really is great to have some contact with the outside world."

Debbie gave her a handshake like a dead fish and Jessie was surprised to be on the receiving end of a very thin-lipped smile. "Yes, I know who you are. And I saw you in the hot tub with my husband."

Jessie took back her hand, smiling uncertainly.

"We showed Debbie the tapes from last night," said Lois. "We just wanted to keep her up to speed."

Jessie told herself to keep smiling as Debbie, giggling and blushing, shook hands with Nick. Maybe no one else had noticed Debbie's frosty demeanor. Maybe Jessie had even imagined it.

His wife distracted, Malcolm leaned over to Jessie. "Oops, looks like we were a bit naughty last night."

Jessie drew away. "No, we weren't," she said, annoyed. She tapped her chest. "For goodness' sakes, I was the one who went to bed!"

She swallowed dryly as heads turned.

"So great to have you here, Debbie," she said weakly as Debbie sniffed and walked over to thread a proprietary arm through her husband's.

Jessie tried not to sigh as she went over to put some more sticks on the fire. She would have given anything to be at work right now, where her biggest problem would be a cantankerous computer system or Mrs. Cookson getting into a huff because Jessie wouldn't let her check out books from the reference section. She poked at the fire, missing her friends more than ever.

She straightened up and frowned as Cindi let out a delighted squeal.

Jessie turned to see what everyone was looking at and she tensed as she spotted another rowboat pulling up on shore. She squinted, blinking against the sunlight, at the two figures in the boat.

One got off.

Tall, fair-haired, wearing a cream linen suit. He waved up at them.

Jessie put her hand up to her mouth. "Oh no," she whispered.

Beside her, Cindi stopped jumping up and down and made a moue. "I don't know him," she complained.

Jessie felt Lois's hands on her shoulders.

"Surprise!" said Lois, pushing her forward.

Out of the corner of her eye Jessie could see Kenny circling around to film her reaction and she forced her mouth into a smile which she knew didn't reach her eyes.

"Who is he?" said Nick as the man hurried up the beach.

Jessie tried to answer. "He's...he's..."

Lois pushed Jessie forward again as the man reached them, spreading his arms to pull her into a hug. Jessie stared blankly over his shoulder as Lois answered Nick's question.

"He's Jessie's fiancé."

NICK WAS ABSOLUTELY dumbfounded. He watched Jessie and the man hugging and he could feel the temperature of his blood rising.

Jessie pulled away and turned. "Everyone," she said. "This is Tom Kennedy."

Nick stared at her, waiting for her to refute what Lois had said. She didn't. Apparently, this man with pale blond hair flopping boyishly over his forehead was exactly who Lois said he was.

Nick shook his hand. "You're Jessie's fiancé?" He had to check. He couldn't help thinking that this must be some kind of joke or setup and he was waiting for the punch line.

"That's right," said Tom. "And I'm a big fan of yours. Thanks for taking such good care of my girl."

He twitched as Nick's grip tightened and Nick released his hand before he did any permanent damage.

"No problem," said Nick lightly. He turned his head and

stared into Jessie's eyes, his gaze uncompromising and demanding.

To his amazement, she didn't even look embarrassed. If anything, her expression was defiant. *What's it to you?* said her eyes.

Nick looked away, wondering if he was dreaming.

He'd only just managed to convince himself that her outburst at Cindi the previous night had been nothing more than a drunken flash of temper but there was no explaining this new development.

To find out that she had a boyfriend would be bad enough, but a fiancé? It was inexcusable.

Cindi stepped forward, shaking Tom's hand warmly. "We've heard so much about you," she said. "Not!" She grinned at Jessie. "I can't believe it. You're such a dark horse. Why didn't you tell us about this?"

Jessie laughed gaily. "Oh, everyone's got their secrets." Her eyes flicked to Nick's. "Haven't they?"

He turned away, telling himself to stay calm. So that's how she was going to play it. He was so angry with her he wasn't sure he'd be able to hide it. He would never have slept with her if he'd known she was involved with someone else.

He probed at his bubbling emotions, wondering if that was all it was—anger at being deceived. What else could it be? Hurt that there was someone else in her life? Why should he care—he hardly knew her. That much was painfully obvious.

Cindi, on the other hand, seemed to have forgiven Jessie completely for their tiff. Then again, maybe she didn't even remember it. She'd practically been sleepwalking by the time he'd gotten her back to her shelter and maneuvering her into it, with her limbs flopping everywhere, had been a major effort.

Lois cleared her throat. "Sorry, Cindi. We were planning

to bring your mother here but there was some problem with the flight or visa or something." Lois rolled her eyes. "Red tape! But we did try."

"Oh, no, that's too bad." Cindi's disappointment was embarrassingly fake. "Never mind. Nick can be *my* date for the evening."

Nick smiled weakly. Perfect.

JESSIE PULLED BACK the front of Tom's suit to check the label inside.

"Armani?" she said. She indicated their surroundings. "You're wearing a linen Armani suit—to the beach?"

"What was I supposed to wear?" he laughed. "Hawaiian shirt and Bermuda shorts? Besides, I don't think you're in any position to preach to me."

Jessie looked down at her dress. She had gotten so used to the flimsy garment, it felt completely natural to her. She was almost saddened at the thought of going back to blouses and fitted skirts.

"Everyone's sent their best wishes," said Tom.

Jessie smiled.

"We're all amazed that you're doing so well."

Her smile slipped a notch. She couldn't help analyzing his comment. Why was it so amazing? Had so many people automatically expected her to fail?

She stole a glance at Malcolm and Debbie who were walking up the beach ahead of herself and Tom. Their arms were entwined and they were talking animatedly, their heads close together.

In sharp contrast Jessie couldn't think of a thing to say to Tom, or at least, nothing she wanted to say on camera.

She'd been blindsided by his arrival and more than a little upset by Lois's proclamation that he was her fiancé.

True, Tom *had* proposed to her—but it had been as she was

getting on the plane to the island and it had caught her completely by surprise, especially since they'd only been dating for three months.

She hadn't answered, and apparently he'd taken that as a yes.

Under normal circumstances she would have cleared it up straight away but somehow the surprise on Nick's face had been a balm to her wounded pride and, well, she hadn't denied it.

And now, as every minute passed, she didn't see how she could.

"This is so strange," Tom enthused as they reached the camp. "I've never been here, yet it's all so familiar. I already know my way around."

Jessie pointed to their improvised kitchen. "This is where we keep the green coconuts—they're the ones with milk inside, and over there we have the dry ones, that Nick found further along the beach. They're the ones where—"

"—the milk has turned firm inside," finished Tom. "You can eat it."

"That's right," said Jessie tightly. She was a little irritated that he'd interrupted her, but of course he would have been watching her on the show. He was bound to know stuff.

"Our shelters are over here," she said, leading the way.

"Wow, they look bigger on camera. Are you sure there's going to be room for the two of us?"

Jessie lowered her head as her eyes widened instinctively in alarm. She hadn't even considered that.

"What am I saying?" he laughed. "You've already tested that, haven't you?"

Jessie looked at him quickly, but his tone didn't seem to be accusatory.

Tom glanced over at the others. Malcolm and Debbie were giggling beside Malcolm's shelter and Cindi and Nick were sitting by the campfire. Tom put his hand on Jessie's arm and pulled her towards the nearby grove of trees.

"Look," he said, lowering his voice. "Everyone knows you shared Nick's shelter on the first night and there's been a lot of stuff about the two of you on the Web site."

Jessie fidgeted uncomfortably.

Tom looked embarrassed as he went on. "I'm just saying, that if anything happened, you know, it's okay. I'll understand that it was just an island thing."

Jessie frowned.

Jeepers, she thought, if my true love slept with someone else, *I* wouldn't be able to forgive and forget. Her gaze flicked to Nick and Cindi, hollowing coconuts companionably by the fire. A lump rose in her throat and she swallowed angrily. Well, maybe this just went to show what a genuine and decent man Tom actually was.

She looked into his searching gaze and then shook her head with a touch of impatience.

"Of course nothing happened," she said. "For goodness' sakes, Tom, we're on camera here all the time." She paused. "Or microphoned at least." She reached out and tugged the front of his shirt. "Like you are right now. Nobody could do anything. Not that any of us would want to. Don't be silly."

His mouth widened in a smile and he nodded. "I'm really glad to hear that. I knew I could trust you."

Jessie told her conscience to go take a hike. She smiled at Tom and didn't flinch when he leaned forward and kissed her.

JESSIE WAS AMUSED to see both Debbie and Tom picking unenthusiastically at their dinner. They obviously hadn't been hungry long enough for leftover roast pig and flaky potato cakes to be appetizing.

The four natives were tucking in with relish.

Jessie had successfully managed to avoid any real conversation with Tom all afternoon because she kept distracting him with island stuff: the raft, the tiki hut, their failed attempt to build a shower. She taught him how to poke the coconuts with the long bamboo poles until they dropped. She showed him how they'd made a frame for smoking fish over the fire and she demonstrated how to distill seawater.

Her diversions brought them up to dinnertime and as the dinner progressed she was becoming more and more impenitent that she had acknowledged Tom as her fiancé.

Nick, who had avoided them all afternoon, was wholeheartedly blanking her now. She could understand his pique—even she could see that it was flagrantly inappropriate of her to produce a fiancé out of thin air—but it wasn't like Nick himself was so squeaky clean. In fact, he'd been a jerk *first*.

So she was ignoring him right back and nodding with interest as Debbie regaled them with pregnancy and real estate anecdotes.

"So it did take us some time to find the perfect house, but we wanted to be sure because we knew that once we did find it, we'd be able to concentrate fully on having babies." Debbie patted her slight bump.

"So if you win the money you're not planning to move," asked Cindi with incredulity.

Debbie and Malcolm looked at each other and shook their heads in unison.

"It's a really nice community and our next-door neighbors have the sweetest two-year-old." Debbie looked around until she found Kenny. She waved into the camera.

"Hi, Carl and Nancy. And, hi, Melissa, if you're watching. You should be in bed!"

"Would you move if you won the money?" Malcolm asked Cindi.

She looked thoughtful. "Hmm, move out of my fleabag apartment and leave behind my insane roommate who never cleans up after herself and hangs her underwear everywhere? That's a tough one." She nodded dramatically, laughing. "Yeah, I probably would."

Then she froze and her eyes drifted towards the camera. "Er, and by insane, I mean of course that she's a very sweet person."

She covered her face with her hand and groaned in embarrassment, tilting sideways to bury her face on Nick's shoulder. He patted her head.

"There, there," he laughed. "I'm sure she won't have changed the locks by the time you get back."

Jessie dropped her eyes, picking at a potato cake. It incensed her that Nick and Cindi weren't even trying to disguise the fact that they were a couple. No wonder Nick hadn't wanted to tell the world that he'd slept with Jessie, he'd had someone better lined up.

"We're not planning to move if Jessie wins the money, are we, honey?" said Tom. He chuckled. "Although we're probably going to have some arguments about which house we're going to live in."

Jessie joined in with a hollow chuckle, focusing on her potato cake again. She wished Tom would stop talking about them in the plural.

She hadn't thought about moving at all—not for money and certainly not to go and live with someone else. But the alternative was Tom coming to live with her; no, she'd have to put some more thought into it.

She hadn't really made any plans for what she'd do with the money if she won. She'd like a new car and there were lots of repairs needed at home—and she'd buy a new boiler for her grandparents. Heck, maybe they'd like a new house.

And of course she'd buy stuff for all her friends and colleagues at the library.

Then, when she'd made sure that everyone she loved was taken care of, would it be too dissolute to spend the rest on holidays? She had a lot of wasted time to make up for. She could go to all those places that she'd only ever read about.

She finished off the last of her food and took a refill of water from Tom.

Honeymoon. That was a trip she'd be taking whether she won or not.

"Would you like to see the Great Barrier Reef, in Australia?" she blurted to Tom.

He looked at her in surprise and Debbie looked affronted. Jessie smiled abashedly, realizing she'd interrupted another pregnancy yarn.

"Sure," answered Tom. "Sounds like fun."

"You should make sure to have a few diving lessons before you go," suggested Nick. "It's really the only way to experience the full wonder of it."

He stopped abruptly as Jessie looked at him. Their eyes locked and Jessie's heart flittered painfully. For one moment they'd forgotten and had gone back to the day by the lagoon, when they were sharing their interests and experiences. Nick looked away and the intimacy vanished as quickly as it had appeared. Jessie realized that it really was over between them, that there was no going back.

But it didn't matter because she had Tom now. It was just a matter of familiarizing herself with him again. After all, their afternoon together had been pleasant and there'd been quite a few moments when she hadn't thought of Nick at all.

Tom was sweet and attentive. A little overprotective sometimes but that was hardly a bad thing. He had a good, steady job at the bank—as soon as Mr. Burton retired Tom would be manager.

And Tom was undeniably attractive. He was handsome and clean-cut in a way that Nick could never hope to be.

Oops, there she went comparing him to Nick again. Okay, so Tom wasn't an adventurous, outdoor, rugged man, but this was the twenty-first century wasn't it? Nobody *needed* to be like that.

So Tom couldn't navigate by the stars or trap a bear or improvise a fuse out of a chewing gum wrapper. He knew how to call an electrician, didn't he?

A tangential thought struck her. If it came to something like that, *she* knew how to call an electrician. And Nick would know that about her.

She realized she was chewing at her fingernail when Tom took her hand in his, lifting his eyebrows in affectionate admonishment.

"You two are so cute," said Debbie. "How long have you been together?"

"I guess it's a whirlwind romance," said Tom. "What is it, honey, about three months?"

"Jessie is a fast mover," said Nick blandly.

Jessie fired a look at him. She was about to make a smart comment about some people being happy with *one* partner, but then she remembered that she couldn't exactly claim the moral high ground in that regard. She clamped her mouth shut and looked down at the fire.

"And how did you propose?" asked Debbie, beaming at Tom. "I bet it was romantic."

Jessie's conscience gave her another sharp nudge and she gave in. She squeezed Tom's hand and spoke up.

"Uh, the thing is, the proposal was kind of sudden..." She trailed off, aware that everyone was staring at her with avid interest.

Tom was looking at her doubtfully, but she forced herself to go on, her voice getting tinier with each word.

"The thing is, Tom, that I didn't actually give you an answer."

She could see everyone glancing at each other and she mentally cursed her stupid, persistent conscience. Why hadn't she waited until they were alone? Tom really didn't deserve this.

He released her hand and Jessie brought it back to her lap, feeling terrible.

"You're right," said Tom, standing up and reaching into his jacket pocket.

For one crazy moment Jessie thought he was going to pull out a gun, but he produced a small velvet box.

"I was going to save this until we were alone," he said, opening the box and going down on one knee in front of her.

Jessie stared at the huge solitaire diamond ring, glittering and sparkling in the firelight. She breathed in sharply, her breath catching in her throat.

"Jessie Banks, will you do me the honor of becoming my wife?"

Jessie couldn't take her eyes off the ring. It was like a meteor, heading straight for her.

She blinked and eventually looked up at Tom, at his pale blue eyes and hesitant, hopeful smile.

She breathed out.

"Yes, I will."

10

JESSIE DIDN'T KNOW where to look as everyone around the fire broke into applause. She concentrated on the ring as Tom slid it onto her finger. The multifaceted diamond seemed garish in comparison to the natural beauty of the island. Despite the iridescent sparkle it looked incongruous and fake.

Tom put his hands on either side of her face and drew her towards him. He kissed her gently. "I love you," he murmured, gazing into her eyes.

Jessie held his gaze for a moment, then drew back, covering her embarrassment with a smile. She held out her hand, focusing on the ring again.

"Now *that's* what I call a rock," said Cindi, leaning over to admire it.

As Debbie and Cindi cooed over the ring, Jessie took a quick look at Nick. He was poking at the fire, his eyes down, his face unreadable.

Jessie sat back and Tom put his arm around her shoulder as Malcolm told them the story of his proposal to Debbie.

Jessie wasn't listening. Her stomach was fluttering with anxiety. No, she told herself, it's not anxiety, it's excitement. You're excited because you've just agreed to marry a wonderful man. A man who's kind and reliable and well respected and very good-looking. You're going to be so happy together in Fairbury, raising kids in a community where you're both well known and loved.

She glanced sideways at Tom and he gave her a squeeze on the shoulder and a smile. See, Tom was definitely not the kind of guy who would sleep with you and then go off with someone else on the very same night.

Tom had followed her all the way to the Tropics, hadn't he? That was love.

DEBBIE HAD BEEN TRYING to drag Malcolm off to bed for half an hour, but Jessie wouldn't let them go.

"And are there good schools in your neighborhood?" persisted Jessie. "Have you picked one yet?"

"Uh...not yet," said Debbie. "We're taking things one step at a time." Her arm was laced through Malcolm's and Jessie could see her giving surreptitious little tugs.

"Well," said Malcolm. "I think my wife and I could use some sleep."

Every other time he'd tried to leave Jessie had pinned them down with more questions but this time she took pity on them and let them go.

And then there were four.

It's just because of the abnormality of the situation, Jessie told herself. That's why I'm trying to avoid going to bed with the man I've agreed to marry. What I'm feeling is just normal stress, aggravated by tiredness and lack of nutrition. Probably.

Tom gave her another squeeze on the shoulders and Jessie stiffened.

"I guess we'd better get to bed, too," he said. "I'll have to face it sooner or later. Don't worry, I'll protect you from lizards."

Jessie smiled weakly. She must really be stressed if a little joke like that could get on her nerves.

Tom got to his feet and put out his hand, pulling Jessie up beside him.

"Good night, all," he said. "Sleep well."

"We will," said Cindi, smiling up at them.

Jessie tried to quash her jealousy as she and Tom walked up to the shelters. She consoled herself that Cindi was making a mistake by being so brazen about herself and Nick. Sure, she had him now but the chances were that as soon as they were off the island he'd be moving on to the next woman. At least Jessie's humiliation hadn't been laid bare to the public. That was something to be grateful for.

That, and having a wonderful, handsome man of her very own.

Yes, thought Jessie, as they reached the shelter, I'm definitely the winner here.

She lit the lamp she'd made out of her perfume bottle.

Tom peered at it. "Is perfume flammable?"

Jessie shrugged. "I don't know. Maybe. I filled it with kerosene."

"Oh, that's right," nodded Tom. "Your bag of tricks."

She frowned quizzically.

"That's what they call it on the Web site." He smiled as he took off his shoes. "Who would have thought you could be so resourceful?"

Jessie decided to ignore her pang of resentment at his comment. She was tired, it had been a long day. She stroked her bare arm absently, realizing that this was the first night that she was going to bed without Nick's T-shirt.

"Are these things as uncomfortable as they look?" Tom said jovially as Jessie showed him how to lift up the roof.

"They're not so bad," she said, matching his tone. "It helps that we're always so tired at the end of the day."

They climbed into the bed and Tom settled the roof over them. He leaned out and blew out the lamp. "Let's have some privacy," he said. He lay down on his side and pulled Jessie towards him, one arm under her neck and the other around her waist. His fingers pressed into the small of her back as he pulled her against him.

He kissed her gently and Jessie responded until his kiss grew more fervent, his lips trying to part hers.

She pulled back with an awkward laugh.

"We can't really do anything here," she said. "You're forgetting about the cameras."

"There aren't any in the shelters, are there?" he said, peering up at the roof.

"Well, no," she admitted, shifting so that there was a bit of space between them. "But the others will hear us. Sounds really carry here at night."

"Oh, they won't take any notice," he said, pulling her into him again. "They'd expect it." His mouth searched for hers.

Jessie put her hand on his chest, pulling her head back. "I really wouldn't feel comfortable."

"We could take a walk down to the beach," he suggested. "Find ourselves a secluded spot."

"No such thing," she reminded him. "There are cameras everywhere. And anyway, I'm pretty tired. We really should get some sleep."

He let out a sigh of frustration. "I guess you're right. But I've just missed you so much."

"Me, too," muttered Jessie awkwardly. She'd only slept with Tom once, and while it had been pleasant, it wasn't exactly honest of her to say she'd *missed* it.

But that was a train of thought she didn't want to get on.

Tom grunted as he moved about, trying to get comfortable. He pulled twigs and leaves out from under him and Jessie let out a squeak as he caught her hair under his elbow.

"Sorry," he said. "Listen, do you mind if I sleep on my left side? I think it's a bit softer here near the edge."

"Sure," said Jessie, turning as he did.

It should have been a comfort to have her back pressed up against Tom's, but Jessie couldn't help feeling a petty irritation that he was taking up most of the space in the shelter.

She gazed out through a gap in the side of the shelter, catching a glimpse of the stars in the dark sky. She was probably just tired, that's why she was so cranky. Things would be much better in the morning.

"I'm so glad you agreed to marry me, Jessie," came Tom's voice in the darkness. "I really love you."

"Mmm," said Jessie sleepily. She waited a moment and then added a few soft fake snores for good measure.

"IT LOOKS TOO DANGEROUS," said Debbie nervously.

"It'll be fine, honey," said Malcolm.

If she says that again, thought Jessie, I'm just going to push her over the edge.

Morning hadn't found Jessie in any better mood than the night before. In fact, she'd woken stiff and cramped from being squashed uncomfortably by Tom all night.

With the result that everything and everyone seemed to be getting on her nerves. Tom was so eager to join in with island life that Jessie was wondering sardonically if he was planning to move to the Tropics altogether. Unfortunately, Debbie's twittering nervousness was just as infuriating.

And to her amazement, Nick seemed determined to maintain the moral high ground; as if the fact that Jessie had a fiancé was so much more egregious than sleeping with two women in the one day. Jessie couldn't fathom how he was justifying that to himself.

"Don't worry," Cindi joined Malcolm in reassuring Debbie. "Nick knows what he's doing."

Jessie barely refrained from snorting. Instead she went over to the edge of the cliff again and peered down. Nick was almost at the bottom.

Since they were entertaining guests on the island Nick had explained that, instead of a challenge, they would simulate a real-life survival situation whereby a stranded group of people—say, from a plane crash—had to cross a dangerous river in their trek to civilization. The river in question also happened to be at the bottom of a cliff.

Nick had tied a rope to a sturdy pandanus tree and was scaling down the cliff face. He was going to cross the river and then fix the rope to a tree at the other side. The plan was that they would all slide down in a harness affixed to a pulley. They were very nervous and excited about it, except for Debbie who was just plain nervous and growing more so by the minute, though she wasn't participating.

Jessie watched as Nick reached the bottom and then she drew back quickly as he looked up. She regretted it immediately, feeling childish.

"He's at the river," she told the others and Tom and Cindi joined her on the cliff edge. They could see Nick studying the river and after a moment he walked north along the bank before starting to wade in. He struck out and swam with powerful strokes but the river was strong and the current carried him. He progressed diagonally, slow but steady.

"Ooh," said Cindi, wrapping her arms around herself. "Be careful, Nick."

Jessie chewed at her lip, pretty sure that he wasn't in any real danger.

"He should have gone in farther down," said Tom. "Away from that bend. The current wouldn't be so strong."

Jessie turned her head slowly to look at him.

Cindi, on the other side, was gazing up at him with trepidation in her eyes. "Really?" she said, alternating her gaze between Nick and Tom.

"Yes, really?" said Jessie archly. "You have a lot of experience with crossing rivers, do you?"

Tom grinned and put an arm across her shoulder, squeezing her. "Probably not as much as you, my little adventurer."

Jessie opened her mouth, then closed it and looked away

in disbelief. What she'd been about to say probably wasn't suitable for television anyway.

She fumed silently as Nick reached the opposite bank and pulled himself out, giving them a cheery wave as he set about tying the rope to a strong tree. Tom and Cindi were staring over the edge and Jessie studied Tom's back for a moment. She'd never paid any attention to it before but she and Tom were exactly the same height. She thought she might even be half an inch taller. She didn't know what irked her more; being called a *little* adventurer or the fact that Tom was acting as if *he'd* survived seven days on the island.

Nick had affixed the rope and he was shaking it vigorously to remove the last spray of water and, presumably, to see if it was going to hold.

He shouted up at them and they all looked at each other, wondering who was going to go first.

"I guess I'll take the plunge," said Malcolm bravely.

Debbie clutched at his arm. "No," she said, in a rather shrill voice. "Er, I mean, doesn't anyone else want to go first?"

"I'll do it!" Cindi said impulsively. "If I have to watch someone else, I'll lose my nerve."

She strapped the harness around herself and stood, jittering, while Jessie double-checked that it was done up correctly. Cindi sat down on the edge of the cliff and held onto the rope that came down to the front of the harness.

"Any last words?" said Kenny, zooming in on her face.

Jessie gave him a light slap on the shoulder. "Kenny! That doesn't help." She looked down at Cindi. "You'll be fine. Just go for it."

Cindi nodded and inched her bottom out along the stone. One minute she was on the cliff and the next she had disappeared, leaving only a high-pitched squeal behind.

They all gasped as she went hurtling down the rope and

flew straight into Nick's arms at the bottom. Huge grins of relief broke out on their faces as she waved excitedly and yelled at them while Nick unstrapped her.

Tom hoisted the harness back up along the rope and Malcolm looked questioningly at Debbie.

"Cindi's so light," Debbie said fretfully. "Will it hold a man's weight?" She raised her eyebrows pointedly at Tom.

Tom looked dissatisfied. "I don't want to leave Jessie."

She was about to tell him not to be so silly but Debbie interrupted. "Oh, Jessie could go. She's bigger than Cindi."

Jessie's nose flared. How charming.

"Okay," she said tightly. "See you all on the ground."

She put on the harness and sat on the cliff-edge. Wow, it really was something when you were about to go. Nick and Cindi looked very small and it went against all her natural instincts to inch farther and farther off the edge. Taking a deep breath, she pushed herself into space.

The river came hurtling towards her at a frightening speed. Wind whipped her hair back and she let out a yell that was half elation, half terror. Above her she could hear the rattle of the pulley as it shot along the rope.

Amazingly, as she neared the ground her weight pulled the rope downwards so she was no longer falling vertically but zooming along horizontally until it brought her crashing into Nick.

His arms closed around her and she felt his whole body hard against hers. Her arms were around his neck and she could smell him, clean and wet from the river. The wet of his clothes seeped into her own and for one vivid moment Jessie realized that she wanted nothing more than to stay molded against him and never let him go.

"Isn't it fantastic!" yelled Cindi next to her. Nick's eyes broke from hers and Jessie felt a sharp physical disappointment.

I Will Survive

She looked down, fumbling with the buckles of the harness as she untangled herself. Nick took it from her without touching her and waved at the others to pull it back up.

Jessie felt winded, and not from the harrowing descent. Her insides were knotted with regret and anger and jealousy and she wanted to yell out loud with vexation. For a little while she'd managed to convince herself that she'd gotten over Nick, that it had been nothing but a silly crush but how was she supposed to deal with the fact that her whole body still ached for him?

She looked back up to the top of the cliff and tried to concentrate on the sight of Debbie fussing over Malcolm as she triple-checked the harness before letting him go.

Released at last, Malcolm made it down with equal aplomb. Nick laughed and congratulated him as Malcolm plucked hopelessly at the harness buckle with trembling fingers.

Jessie looked to the top of the cliff. She had no choice but to get over Nick. He'd made his position clear and she was in danger of losing a perfectly good man just because of some crazy hormonal vacillating.

Tom was pulling the harness up along the rope.

"It's okay, sweetheart," she shouted up, forcing affection into her tone. "We haven't forgotten you. Good luck!"

Tom waved at her as he put on the harness. He sat down and pushed himself off the cliff in one quick movement.

Jessie forced herself to smile encouragingly for the benefit of the Island Eyes, but it quickly turned to a look of dismay as Tom let out a panicked yell. Jessie watched in horror as the strap around one of his legs snapped open, leaving him swinging precariously, even as he continued to hurtle downwards. Jessie's hands flew to her face and Cindi gasped as Tom let go of the harness with one hand to reach for the leg strap. He seemed to be swinging wildly and Jessie prayed frantically that he'd reach the ground before the other strap gave.

Seconds stretched like hours and Jessie had stopped breathing by the time Tom reached them, crashing into the ground and rolling over a few times before scrambling to his feet, laughing.

"Whoa," he said. "Now, *that's* what I call nerve-wracking."

Nick's face was creased with consternation as he helped Tom remove the harness.

"I don't understand it," he muttered, examining the straps. "I checked this."

"Don't worry about it," said Tom. "I think the strap just came loose or something. No harm done." He grinned and pulled Jessie into a hug. "Are you okay, darling? You're white as a sheet."

"That was terrifying," she said, exhaling as she hugged him.

Tom dipped his head and whispered into her ear. "I know. Good television, eh?"

Jessie pulled back her head and looked at him.

He winked at her.

Jessie frowned and pulled out of his embrace. "You said the strap came loose?" she asked warily.

He answered in a complicit undertone. "With a little bit of help."

Jessie's mouth fell open. "You're kidding?"

He answered with a mischievous smile, looking childishly pleased with himself.

"What were you thinking?" snapped Jessie. "You could have been killed!"

Tom looked peeved. "Take it easy. I knew what I was doing."

Jessie shook her head in outrage. "I don't believe this.

Tom, that was incredibly stupid. If it was a real survival situation you would have endangered us all. What if you'd broken your leg or something?"

Tom's gaze softened. "Oh, Jess," he said, putting his hands on her arms. "I didn't mean to scare you. It's okay, I'm safe."

Jessie shrugged off his arms. Then, much as she didn't want to, she added, "You're going to have to apologize to Nick. He's responsible for you here."

"I DON'T WANT TO GO."

Jessie couldn't help sighing, but she pretended it was because she was upset that Tom's sojourn on the island was coming to an end. The truth was that she couldn't wait for him to go.

He'd apologized to Nick for his reckless behavior, but Jessie could still sense that Nick didn't really like him. Not that she was Nick's favorite person, either.

Since Tom had arrived, Jessie felt like she couldn't think straight. Either there were too many people around and Tom's smooth social graces irritated her or else there weren't enough people around and he got on her nerves with his constant hovering and talk about the future.

On the way back from the river he'd been telling her about the newspapers and talk-show hosts who wanted to interview her when the show was over.

"Don't worry," he'd said. "We'll think very carefully about who we pick to talk to."

Jessie hadn't answered. She hadn't wanted to think about it at all.

Now they were watching as the motorboat pulled up on shore, coming to take Tom and Debbie away.

"It's only three more days," Jessie said with an edge in her voice as Tom hugged her again. "We'll see each other soon."

"That's the spirit," he said, stroking her hair.

"Do you want to hear what difference your guests have made to the polls?" Lois teased them as she approached, waving her clipboard tantalizingly. "Or not?"

"I didn't have any guests," wailed Cindi. "Did *that* make a difference?"

"Let's see," said Lois. "Malcolm and Debbie first." She smiled benevolently at the couple and clasped the clipboard to her chest. "Everyone loved you and heartstrings are twanging all over the place at the thought of the new arrival. You're a popular choice with the voters."

Cindi's shoulders slumped as Lois turned to her. "Not much of a change either way for you I'm afraid. But things might improve because Jessie's audience support has taken a major dive."

"What?" said Jessie in outrage.

Lois put up her hand. "Oh, no, not in a bad way. It's just that, well, they think you've got everything you need. You've got looks, a good job and now, a fabulous man. General consensus seems to be, why should she get the money as well?"

Lois looked at Tom, even though she was still talking to Jessie. "You silly girl—it wasn't very clever of you to have such a handsome fiancé."

Jessie stared at her. Ye gods, she thought, is Lois *flirting*? It was as disturbing as seeing a vulture use cutlery.

"In fact," Lois went on, referring to the pages in front of her, "thirty-one percent of women aged 25 to 40 think that Jessie doesn't deserve him." Lois glanced at Tom and winked. "You've got yourself some fans out there."

Jessie watched as Tom dipped his head bashfully and then brushed back the lock of hair that fell forward. "You hear that, sweetheart?" he said with an endearing smile. "Maybe I can do better than you."

Jessie retorted without thinking. "Hey, you want someone else," she snapped, "go for it."

He laughed, dropping a playful kiss on her unyielding lips. "Don't be a jealous kitten. You know you're my one and only."

"You *are* a lucky girl," Cindi joined in. "I'd snap him up myself in an instant."

Of course you would, thought Jessie bitterly. I'm sure that taking one man from me wasn't enough.

She took a deep breath and suddenly it seemed as if the moment froze for a perfect snapshot in her mind.

Nick was talking quietly to Kenny, both of them examining the camera casing.

Malcolm and Debbie were murmuring to each other, sharing their last endearments before Debbie was taken away.

And Tom was preening and basking in the attention of the two women who were giggling and flirting with him.

In that very moment Jessie realized why Tom had been so very helpful in getting her a replacement flight after she'd deliberately missed her first one. His proposal at the airport, his being here now, none of it had anything to do with her. He just wanted to grab some of the fame and attention. The whole time he'd been here he'd been putting her down and patronizing her—much as he did at home. She'd never noticed it before because she'd always assumed that he was right and that his advice was constructive and necessary.

But here, things were different. She might not know very much about life on an island but she knew a damn sight more than him.

Jessie took another breath, feeling her head clear. What on earth had she been thinking? How could she ever have thought that this would work?

Her smile faded as Lois clicked her fingers impatiently at Kenny, telling him not to miss the final goodbyes.

Jessie chewed at her lip. I can't dump him now, she thought as Tom enveloped her in a hug. I'll look stupid and heartless.

After all, she still had to spend three more days around Nick and Cindi. An imaginary fiancé was better than nothing. She'd tell Tom first thing when she got home, in private.

"Come on, you two," said Lois. "Break it up. It's time to go." She patted Jessie on the arm. "Never mind. Having a dreamboat of a fiancé may have cost you the money, but at least you got to have some fun with him here on the island. Your man is quite a daredevil, isn't he?"

Again, Lois was ostensibly talking to Jessie, but her attention was on someone else.

Tom laughed, showing a gleaming white smile. "Maybe I should have been the contestant, not my little Jessie. I might have had a better chance of winning the money."

Jessie breathed in deeply.

There it was, the proverbial last straw.

"You know what, Tom?" she said, her voice rising gradually. "Why don't you take a good hard look at me? I am not a jealous kitten, I am not your *little* adventurer and I am not your *little* Jessie. I'm taller than you, you idiot!"

Jessie looked down, wrenching at the engagement ring.

"Here, take your ring and get off my island!" The ring went whizzing past Tom's shoulder and landed in the sand, some distance from them.

Tom, true to form, went running after it.

"That's a two-carat diamond," he yelled over his shoulder as he scrambled in the sand. "Do you have any idea how much it cost?"

"Go fetch," she said happily, storming off in the opposite direction.

"LEAVE ME ALONE."

"I'd like to," said Nick with annoyance, "but Lois told me to get you."

Jessie was huddled in her shelter, arms folded over her

knees. She glared crossly at Nick who had tilted up the roof so he could look in at her.

"Is he gone?" said Jessie. "I don't want to see him."

"Lois has just put them on the boat."

"I'm surprised she doesn't want me to do the scene again," Jessie said sourly, "so that Kenny can get a better angle on it." She put her head down on her arms. "What a mess."

Nick snorted derisively.

Jessie looked up. "Excuse me?"

"Oh, please," he said. "Don't try putting on an act for me. You knew exactly what you were doing. You were plummeting in the audience votes, so you simply made it interesting again. You've probably won the support of all the independent, single women out there in one fell swoop."

"How dare you," she said. She was infuriated by the crack in her voice. "This isn't a game, you know, this is my life."

Nick laughed coldly. "Yeah, right. It's your life. Give me a break. You could teach Cindi a thing or two about acting." He looked away, shaking his head. "You may have fooled the others, but I can see that you're doing this for the money, plain and simple. And you don't care who you have to use to get it."

Jessie cried out in exasperation. "What on earth is your problem?"

"My problem?" he snapped back. "My problem is that you had a fiancé. I would never have slept with you if I'd known that. You used me."

"*I* used *you?*" Jessie exclaimed. "You're unbelievable! Just leave me alone."

"My pleasure."

11

"PLEASE. I'M BEGGING YOU."

"Don't be silly," Lois said again. "You don't *really* want to go home."

Jessie groaned in exasperation. "Yes, I really do."

"Well, you can't." Apparently, Lois had had enough of mollycoddling. "Besides, it's practically your last day. Stop being such a baby."

"You can't keep me here against my will."

"What are you going to do, swim? Go ahead. Or why don't you take Nick's raft?" mocked Lois. "Look," she said, adopting a woman-to-woman tone. "I know you're in a panic now because you blew it with Tom, but running after him is not the way to go, trust me. Remember, 'treat 'em mean, keep 'em keen.' Besides, you're in with a chance of winning again."

"I don't care about Tom," said Jessie.

"There you go," Lois praised her. "I'd almost believe you myself. Keep that up and then maybe tomorrow at the last minute you could confess that you really do miss him." Lois tilted her head, musing speculatively. "Maybe say something about giving up the money if only you could have him back. Although, that's a risk—you might end up having to give it away." Lois shrugged as Jessie looked at her, disturbed. "I dunno, I'm just throwing out some ideas here. My point is, you can't give up, the game's not over yet."

Jessie put her hand to her forehead. "Why does everyone keep saying that this is a game?"

Lois ignored her as she listened with a cross expression to a stream of chatter from her walkie-talkie.

"I don't even know why I'm here in the first place," muttered Jessie. She looked at Lois and asked her point-blank. "Why *am* I here? Why was I picked?"

Lois stopped snapping instructions into the walkie-talkie and looked at Jessie. "That's easy," she said. "You were supposed to be the prim, repressed librarian who comes to the island, lets her hair down and turns into a voracious sex bomb." Lois clucked her tongue. "I must say I was pretty disappointed with you for a while. I was beginning to wonder if you had any libido at all. But of course, then it became clear. If I had a fiancé like Tom I would have held out, too."

"Well, he's free now," said Jessie snidely. "You can have him."

"Mmm," said Lois unenthusiastically. "He's a bit *yesterday's news* for me. Besides, I'm sure he'll take you back. Just try not to seem so needy. No more talk about running back home, okay?"

Jessie looked at her for a long moment. "I have never met anyone like you before."

"I get that a lot," said Lois, preening. She brought the walkie-talkie up to her mouth. "No!" she barked. "We only need one. They're doing it in turns. Don't make me come out there!"

"SEARCH AND RESCUE," said Nick, beaming at them. He waved his hand behind him, taking in the expanse of the island in one sweep. "Somewhere out there is an injured person and you've got to find them and bring them back. This could involve making a travois to carry them."

"A what?" said Cindi.

"A kind of sled, made out of branches. I showed you early on in the week, remember?"

Cindi groaned.

"And no, Kenny's not allowed to help you." Nick held up a piece of paper. "I don't want you wandering around out there all day, so here's a map. If you haven't found him within forty-five minutes, you're very lost. You can quit at any time by blowing three times on the whistle. I'll come and get you. But I hope that none of you do that because this is, after all, the last challenge. There's a lot to it, I admit. It'll test your map-reading abilities, tracking skills, first-aid skills; all the stuff I've been teaching you during the week, so I hope you were paying attention."

"What's the point of me doing it?" asked Cindi. "I'm too far behind to win anyway."

"Are you?" said Malcolm. "I thought you and Jessie were even."

They all started talking at the same time, trying to recap on the score and Nick shushed them. He counted off on his fingers.

"Let's see...Malcolm, you got—"

"I caught the fish and won the obstacle course."

"Two points," said Nick. "And Cindi?"

"The scavenger hunt," she said, still looking as if she couldn't believe it, either.

"One point," said Nick. He didn't look up but kept counting on his hand. "And Jessie got..."

"I got a point for working out how to tackle the pit and I also...I found you at the lagoon." To her dismay, this made Jessie want to cry. She cleared her throat and pretended she had something in her eye.

"Two points," said Nick. He looked up at them again. "The good news is that there's two points going for this challenge. One point for rescuing the guy and one for...well, you'll see."

"For what?" demanded Cindi.

"I guess you'll find out when you win it," Nick teased, smiling at Cindi.

Jessie's urge to cry dissipated rapidly.

Nick picked up a twig and broke it into three pieces—two long and one short. He held them out, hidden in his palm.

"HOW MUCH DO YOU THINK an island costs?" asked Jessie, looking over her shoulder. "Do you think you could get one for a million bucks?"

She nodded as if Kenny had answered. "I know, I know, I'd still need to have money left over to live on. Maybe I could get one for a half mill." She chuckled. "A fixer-upper."

She glanced down at the map. Either it was very easy to read or she was actually getting good at this.

"Okay, I think this is the Y-shaped tree so we're going left. He should be—"

She broke off as they heard a faint cry for help. Jessie looked with glee at the camera. "Found him!"

She put her hand up in triumph.

"Fine," she muttered, high-fiving herself. She raised her voice. "Hang on, I'm coming."

She was glad now that Lois hadn't let her leave. Okay, so she had to endure Nick and Cindi, but it was still a little easier than facing everyone back home while her feelings were in such turmoil. How could nine days have made such a difference? When she'd come here she was a woman who was content with her life, albeit bored occasionally. And now? Now she didn't know what she wanted. Even worse, she'd learned to want things that she couldn't have. And even after all the hardship they'd put up with she was going to miss the island and her daily routines: the first swim of the morning, the occasional long walk along the beach, watching the night come in—it always caught her by surprise—one minute there was a deep orangey-red sunset and the next time she looked up, blackness and stars. Even the bugs or the scratchiness of her bed didn't bother her anymore. She loved going to sleep with the fresh smell of sap and sea air in her nostrils. She loved the comforting whisper of the waves. She loved the...whoa, half-naked men that you found in the forest.

"I'm so glad you're here," said the man. "I fell down that slope and I think I'm hurt."

Jessie couldn't help smiling. "And your shirt fell off?"

The man's eyes flickered. "I was checking to see if anything was broken."

"Whatever you say," said Jessie, taking pity on him.

Trust Lois; anything to pull in the viewers.

"I'm Jessie," she said, kneeling down beside him.

"I'm Mark," he said. "I think I broke my arm."

"How about your legs?"

"They're fine."

"Good." Jessie breathed a sigh of relief. "I won't have to carry you back."

She took Mark's arm and probed his wrist and elbow. No reaction. She lifted his arm.

"Ow!" he yelled convincingly.

"Ooh," she said brightly. "Broken shoulder I'd say. Most likely a hairline fracture of the tibia."

"That's the leg," muttered Kenny.

"Whatever," Jessie muttered back.

She patted Mark on the hand. "I'm going to make a splint for your arm and put it in a sling."

"Okay."

"Are you in shock?"

He hesitated. "I don't know."

Jessie felt his forehead and peered into his eyes. "Probably," she diagnosed. "But I think it'll be quicker to get you fixed up and back to camp than to start making you a cup of tea here."

She looked around. "Now, let's see, a splint." She picked up a branch and broke it to a suitable length.

"This will brace your arm," she said authoritatively, tearing off some thin fibrous strips from a vine.

"You have a lovely chest," she said as she tied the strips of vine around the branch and his arm. "You work out?"

"Er, yes," said Mark.

"And you have very strong arms."

Mark glanced sideways at the camera. "Thanks."

"You seem like a nice man."

"Uh, okay." Mark's tone was doubtful.

"Very masculine and virile."

Mark looked distinctly uneasy. "They just told me to act as if I had an injured arm."

Jessie nodded as she examined his shirt, trying different ways to make a sling out of it. She paused and dropped it in her lap, shaking her head.

"Do you know what would happen if I kissed you, Mark?"

His eyes widened.

"Do you know what would happen to me?" demanded Jessie. "What I'd feel?"

Mark shook his head nervously.

"Nothing! That's what. I could kiss you right here and now, full on the lips and I'd feel nothing. It would be like kissing a tree."

Mark looked at Kenny. "They didn't say anything about—"

"Excuse me, Mark," said Jessie, reaching out to turn the camera back on her. "Look, Tom, I just want you to know that it wasn't about you, okay? And everyone else out there who knows me—you must be wondering who this stranger is and what happened to the real Jessie." She smiled. "I'm sorry I yelled at you, Tom, but I think you know as well as I do that we weren't right for each other. You're a wonderful man and I just know you'll have lots of women throwing themselves at you—probably from all over the world. And everyone else, it's still me, I'm just...I'm more..." She gave up, shaking her head. "I'll explain it all when I get home."

She looked down at her patient. "Sorry about that, Mark."

"I have a girlfriend," he said tersely.

"Of course you do," she said, fixing his shirt into a sling. "And you've got a broken tibia, too. Let's get you back to camp."

JESSIE WATCHED AS KENNY took the tape out of his camera and scribbled her name on it before handing it to Nick.

"What are you going to do with that?" she asked.

"Watch it," said Nick.

Jessie stared at the tape nervously. "I'd rather you didn't. I mean, why do you have to?"

"I just want to have a quick look at your rescue technique," explained Nick.

Jessie waved her hand at Mark. "But look, I brought him back. I thought that was the challenge. To find him and bring him back. And I did."

Nick was examining Mark's arm, manipulating the sling. "Good job," he said. "Although you didn't have to take off his shirt."

Jessie's jaw jutted defensively. "I didn't. He was like that when I found him. Tell him, Mark."

Mark shook off the splint, grabbed his shirt from Nick and put it on quickly. "I'd better get back out there."

Nick watched his hasty retreat. "What did you do to him?"

"I didn't...I..." Jessie spluttered in indignation. "You

know what? Watch the tape. You'll see. I didn't do anything."

She walked off, muttering to herself about men and how unreasonable they were. Cindi was sitting under a coconut tree and Jessie joined her.

"So what did you guys do while I was gone?"

Cindi shrugged. "He asked us some questions about survival—not just here, but in other places, too, and stuff about animals." Cindi made a face. "I didn't have a clue and I bet that's what the other point is for."

Jessie nodded. She felt uncomfortable being alone with Cindi. She really wanted to find out how things were going with Nick but she also dreaded hearing the truth out loud. Besides, Cindi spent so much of her time in fantasyland anyway that Jessie couldn't trust anything she said. It's best not to ask, she kept telling herself.

She glanced over to where Nick was watching the tape on a small video camera. She could see him pressing fast-forward and play, then his brows dipped down. Jessie looked away, cringing.

"He was asking about you as well," said Cindi absently.

Jessie felt a tightening in her chest. "What?"

"Yeah," said Cindi. She waved her hand. "About where you live. And about you and Tom." Cindi looked at her secretively. "What *did* happen, by the way? I've been dying to ask you."

"Oh, it was just one of those things." Jessie couldn't think about Tom now. Nick had been asking questions about her. Maybe he'd had an epiphany, too. Maybe seeing her with Tom had made him realize how much he wanted her.

"So, you think you'll get back together with him?" said Cindi.

"What?" said Jessie, startled by Cindi's perspicacity.

"Tom," prompted Cindi. "You think you'll be able to patch things up?"

Jessie shook her head impatiently. "That's finished. It would never have worked."

"That's too bad."

Jessie darted a sideways look at her. It was unusual for Cindi to care about something other than herself. Was it possible that she was worried? That she viewed Jessie as a threat?

"How are things going with Nick?" asked Jessie bluntly, staring at Cindi.

Cindi looked at her and Jessie tried to identify what was in her eyes. Anxiety? Guilt? Cindi covered her microphone and leaned forward. "I don't really want to say anything on camera," she mouthed.

"Of course not," Jessie mouthed back, feeling a kernel of hope pop open inside her. So there was trouble in paradise.

"How do you get water from a young banana tree?" Nick checked his clipboard. "Cindi, your turn to answer."

She sighed heavily. "How should I know? Stick a straw into the trunk?"

He turned his head. "Jessie?"

She met his eyes and held them for a moment, trying to read him. He hadn't said anything about her behaviour with the hapless Mark and she wasn't going to ask. "Chop it down," she answered. "Leave about three inches above the ground. Hollow out the trunk and it'll fill up with water from the roots. I think."

"Very good," he said.

Cindi poked her tongue out at Jessie. Even though she was ostensibly playacting Jessie could sense genuine pique coming through. It pleased her and strengthened her suspicions.

Not that Nick had shown any signs of warming to her. If

anything, he was more remote and formal than ever but Jessie had decided that this was just defensiveness.

"How do you treat a snakebite?" he asked. "Jessie, your turn."

"Uh, make a small cut in it," she said, "and suck out the venom?"

He made a face. "That's really not a good idea. That's the kind of thing you'd do if you were stranded on your own and didn't have too much chance of survival anyway. Cindi?"

She frowned. "That's what I was going to say."

Nick told them. "It's best just to apply direct pressure to the bite and bandage firmly above and below the wound to localize the venom and then get medical help as quickly as possible. Just as well I didn't ask Malcolm that," he joked. "He's afraid of snakes."

"Ants," corrected Jessie.

Nick raised his eyebrows.

"He's afraid of ants," Jessie repeated. "Remember when we were doing the obstacle course and he thought that the dirt slope was a giant anthill?"

Nick nodded. "Oh, that's right."

He looked down at his clipboard and made a notation. "Next question to you, Cindi. If you're stranded in the wilderness, how can you use your watch to improvise a compass?"

"I am never going to be stranded in the wilderness," Cindi said with irritation. "I do *not* need to know this stuff."

"Is that your answer?"

Cindi rolled her eyes.

"Sorry," said Nick. "Jessie?"

Jessie kept forgetting this. "Point twelve o'clock to the sun and north is then at six o'clock?"

Nick shook his head. "I'm afraid not. In the northern

hemisphere, point the hour hand at the sun. South is halfway between the hour hand and twelve. In the southern hemisphere, point twelve o'clock at the sun and north is halfway between twelve and the hour hand."

Jessie nodded, confused as ever.

"Here's an easy one," said Nick jovially. "First to answer gets it. Good old U.S. of A., Cindi, so no excuses. What city is the home of the football team, the Broncos?"

Jessie paused warily but when Cindi didn't answer, she jumped in. "Denver."

Nick nodded. "Bingo."

Jessie watched him make another notation.

"How was I supposed to know that?" grumbled Cindi. "I'm not a football fan."

"Neither am I," said Jessie thoughtfully. "But Malcolm was talking about them one night. It's his home team."

"Name a constellation that's only visible from the southern hemisphere," said Nick. "Jessie?"

Jessie hesitated, wondering if he was trying to tell her something by bringing up constellations. She caught her bottom lip between her teeth, narrowing her eyes slightly.

"Do you know?" he said. "Or should I pass it over to—"

"Southern Cross," she said. If he was trying to send her a signal, she wasn't getting it.

"Cindi," he said, turning his head again. He laughed. "Don't look so glum, you might know it."

"Sure," said Cindi. "Bring it on."

"What color eyes will Debbie and Malcolm's baby have?"

Cindi threw her hands up in the air. "You've got to be kidding me!" she shrieked. "What am I, psychic?"

Nick turned to Jessie with a quizzical expression.

Jessie nodded slowly, her heart sinking like a stone through a barrel of oil. "Brown," she answered. "Because both Malcolm and Debbie's are brown."

"Very good," said Nick. He smiled consolingly at Cindi. "Sorry."

"These are the dumbest questions I've ever heard," she bickered. "Ask me who's on a particular agent's B-list, or the name of a network president's secretary—something important, for crying out loud!"

Jessie stared at a baby crab scuttling over a nearby mound of seaweed. She wasn't listening. Nick hadn't been asking questions about her because he'd been interested. He was actually asking them questions about each other as part of the challenge—like a test of their observation skills or something.

It was nothing to do with her personally. She'd completely fooled herself because she wanted to believe it so badly. She'd wanted to believe that there was a chance of reconciliation because without him...

She felt her throat close. Without him she had nothing. She couldn't even begin to imagine being with any other man. She was in love with Nick Garrett and she'd blown it. She should have accosted him the day after the hot tub incident and asked him straight about what had happened with Cindi and what he meant by doing that to her. Her stupid pride had kept her from sorting it out and now it was too late.

MALCOLM LOOKED QUITE DRAINED by the time he arrived back, dragging Mark on a travois behind him. Nick checked Mark, took the cassette tape from Kenny and told Cindi to get ready. Mark took off his bandages again and jogged back into the forest. Cindi went to get a bottle of water and some supplies and Malcolm gratefully foraged in their kitchen when Nick told him to get something to eat.

Cindi took the map from Nick with a sigh and set off into

the forest. Nick busied himself looking through his pages of questions and scores while he and Jessie waited for Malcolm.

Jessie looked out at the beach and then back at his down-turned head and then out at the beach again. She chewed at her thumbnail and then turned back, peeking at him out of the corner of her eye.

It would be so easy to just let it go. In two days she'd be back home and she'd never have to see him again. And that was also the reason why she had to talk to him.

"Nick?"

"Yup?" he said curtly, not looking up.

Jessie's heart thumped hard in her chest. "Can we talk?"

His eyes flicked up and he looked at her from under his brows.

Jessie faltered under the forbidding gaze but she wrapped her hand around her microphone anyway, asking him with her eyes to do the same.

He sighed and covered his microphone. He glanced over at Malcolm who was safely out of earshot.

"What's to talk about?" said Nick coldly.

"Look," she said, "we both made mistakes—"

"I know I did," he said snidely. "I made a real big one."

Somehow it didn't sound like an admission of guilt so much as a dig at her, so Jessie didn't stop to analyze it.

"Okay," she continued hastily, "but Tom's gone now and you..."

"What?"

She decided against quizzing him about the current state of his relationship with Cindi, and chose instead to focus on them.

"I miss you," she said softly.

"I'm right here," he retorted rudely.

Jessie exhaled through her nose. "Nick, please. Can't you see that I'm trying to say..."

"What?" he said again.

She looked up, staring into his eyes, trying to find the Nick that she'd fallen in love with. "Don't you know how I feel about you?"

A spark lit his eyes and Jessie caught her breath but then the gates came down again.

"I get it," he laughed cynically. "Your fiancé's gone, so now you're feeling lonely again? What's the matter, you can't survive for two days without a man? And I guess Mark didn't come through for you, either. So, it's back to me. Oh, boy, let's go, I'm all yours."

Jessie looked away, shaking her head in frustration at his refusal to meet her halfway. "It's not like that and you know it."

"Do I, Jessie?"

She looked back, a part of her twanging hopefully as he said her name.

"I thought I knew you," he said. "I really did, but then there was the thing with Cindi—"

"The *thing* with Cindi," Jessie interrupted angrily, "Is that what you call it? Don't tell me, that's changed your perspective utterly, has it?"

"It did make me see things differently," he said, looking uncomfortable.

Jessie shook her head as Malcolm approached them. It was hopeless. "I don't know why I even tried to talk to you," she muttered. "Just forget it."

12

A MILLION DOLLARS, thought Jessie.

A one and six zeroes. That's a lot of money. Enough to make any girl very happy. That's it, focus on the money.

"I can't stand it," said Cindi. "This is unbearable."

"Oh, calm down," said Malcolm. "What's the big deal?"

"The big deal," said Cindi sarcastically, "is that Lois said she'd be here this *morning*. Shouldn't she be here by now? Why are they torturing us like this?"

"What's another few hours?" said Malcolm with a phlegmatic shrug. "We've done the hard part. We should be congratulating ourselves."

"I just know I'm not going to win." Cindi continued to fret. "I didn't try hard enough at the challenges. And I talked about myself too much. It's because I'm an actress, it's part of my job to examine my emotions. That's why so many actors end up together, because we need to be with someone who understands the process." She sighed. "But then you just end up with someone who's as self-obsessed as you are."

Jessie hooted with laughter. "No kidding!"

Cindi looked at her anxiously. "I *did* talk about myself too much, didn't I? Not like you guys. That's why I couldn't answer any of the questions in the last challenge. I don't care that I couldn't answer any survival ones but I couldn't even answer the simple questions about either one of you."

"It doesn't matter about the challenges," Malcolm placated her. "It's audience votes that decide who gets the money."

"Yeah, but who's going to vote for me?" Cindi gnawed at her fingernails. "They'll vote for you, Malcolm, because you're a family man. Or you, Jessie, because you're so nice."

Jessie snorted. Yeah, she thought, *nice* gets you real far in this world.

She was miserable at the thought of leaving the island and disillusioned by her failure to get through to Nick and find some sort of closure to their affair. If you could even call it that. She kept trying to tell herself that he was just a jerk and the sooner she got away from him the better, but her heart couldn't accept what her mind was trying to sell it. Everything she'd seen of Nick over the past ten days argued that he was anything but a jerk.

Okay, apart from the fact that he'd chosen Cindi over her. Surely that at least showed that the guy had no taste.

"Hot shower," said Cindi. "Pizza. Delivered to my door." She closed her eyes and moaned in ecstasy. "These are the things that I can still have whether I win or not. Cable TV."

"Clean clothes," said Malcolm. "Even going back to work will be nice. A lot easier than this. The sports channel. What are you looking forward to, Jessie?"

Jessie hesitated.

Nothing, was the word that immediately sprang to mind.

But she couldn't say that.

Malcolm prompted her as if she hadn't heard him. "Jessie? What did you miss most?"

"My dog, Toby," she said in a rush. "Of course. I can't wait to see him. And all my friends."

"Sleeping comfortably again," laughed Malcolm. "In my own bed."

"Sleep!" said Cindi. "I knew there was something else I missed."

Jessie was staring out towards the cliffs at the far end of the beach, trying to imprint the memory on her brain. A bed, grass, mud hut: what difference did it make to her where she slept, if she wasn't sleeping with Nick?

JESSIE WAS SURPRISED that Cindi had any nails left. When she'd finally arrived, Lois had refused to give them even the slightest hint. She'd just rushed straight into arranging them, making them sit, stand and swap around repeatedly until she was satisfied. In the end she settled for simply seating them in a row on a log: Cindi, Malcolm and Jessie. Lois sat across from them and Nick sat on a tree stump to one side. The contestants each had separate handheld cameras trained on them with Kenny roaming to get other shots.

Despite herself, Jessie's excitement was beginning to build. What on earth would she do if she won?

Lois made sure that all the cameras were rolling and then she smiled expansively at them. She was wearing a shimmering silk blouse and sarong and gold lipstick burnished her lips. Jessie ran her hand through her hair, then wondered why she was bothering.

"I guess you're all on tenterhooks," said Lois. "But I'd like to ask you a few questions first."

Jessie smiled to herself. Lois was really taking her life in her hands, making Cindi wait.

"What was the best part of the experience for you, Cindi?"

Cindi smiled like the actress she was. "Just being here and making such lovely new friends was the best for me. We shared so much on this island and when you go through thick and thin together like we did, it forms a true bond."

Jessie dipped her head, rubbing at her forehead. Great, she thought as the laughter bubbled in her chest, it probably looks like I'm overcome with emotion now. She got a grip on herself and looked up again, nodding along with Cindi.

"Malcolm?" prompted Lois. "What did you learn?"

"More than I could ever describe in a few sentences," said Malcolm solemnly. "I learned that I was capable of pushing myself harder than I would have ever thought and that the mind is the most powerful tool when it comes to survival. I also learned that your family and friends are the most precious thing in your life and you should never take them for granted."

Jessie looked worriedly at the sand in front of her. What was she going to say—that she'd gained *and* lost a fiancé, and worse still, she'd fallen truly in love, and lost him, too. And she was going home with her heart broken into a million tiny pieces.

"Jessie?" said Lois. "What did you gain from your time here?"

Jessie smiled awkwardly. "I just really enjoyed living out in the wild and having adventures and meeting such great people. It was an unforgettable experience."

Lois waited, then shrugged.

"Oh-kay," she said. "Let's get to the good stuff. Do you guys have any idea who won?"

They all looked at each other, shaking their heads. Jessie realized that she really had no idea. They were all so different and the week had been so varied that it was impossible to even take a guess.

"First of all, though," said Lois, "I'm going to tell you who won the challenges."

Cindi let out a groan and then brightened quickly as a camera zoomed in on her.

Lois checked her clipboard. "Cindi, you got one point for the scavenger hunt. Well done."

Cindi waved into the camera, smiling bravely.

"Malcolm, you won the fishing, the obstacle course and you made the quickest rescue yesterday. Three points."

Malcolm nodded modestly, grinning.

"Jessie, you won the pit challenge and tracking Nick and you answered the most general knowledge questions yesterday so it's three for you as well. So, we have a tie." Lois gave them a catlike smile. "Rather than make you fight to the death we've decided to give you both prizes. Malcolm and Jessie, you're going home with brand-new, fully loaded Land Rovers!"

Jessie felt herself pulled into a bear hug from Malcolm and she laughed, hugging him before pushing him off gently. She didn't want him to get in any more trouble with Debbie.

"Congratulations, you guys," squealed Cindi, hugging Malcolm and reaching past him to squeeze Jessie's arm.

"And now, the final result," said Lois portentously.

Jessie licked her lips with nervousness, glancing over at Nick. He looked away quickly, as if she'd caught him watching her.

Lois went on. "You were all great contestants and it was a close call but our audience did vote a winner and that winner is...Cindi!"

Cindi was silent for one second and then she jumped to her feet with an ear-splitting scream.

Jessie felt a quick stab of disappointment, but it was followed by a much larger wave of relief. If she'd won the money her actions and mistakes could have been seen as pure manipulation, rather than honest muddling.

She rose to her feet, smiling and joining in as she and Malcolm hugged Cindi who was crying and gushing her thanks to everyone.

Jessie and Malcolm gave each other a commiserating hug and Jessie was pleased to see that he didn't look too disappointed. She concentrated on patting him on the shoulder so she wouldn't have to watch as Cindi wrapped herself around Nick.

"Thank you so much to everyone who voted for me," Cindi gushed effusively as she turned to the cameras again. "To all my wonderful fans everywhere. I couldn't have gotten through this without your support. Just knowing you were out there watching over me gave me the strength and the courage to go on. I love you all."

Jessie, along with everyone else, couldn't help applauding.

JESSIE WAS PACKING as many mementoes of the island as she could fit into her cloth bag. Shells, the cutlery she'd whittled, shoes she'd woven. She noticed that Malcolm was doing the same thing, but not Cindi. Cindi was making no secret of the fact that she couldn't wait to leave it all behind.

Jessie was trying to concentrate on thinking about her new all-terrain vehicle when Lois came along with Kenny in tow.

"Just want to get a few final words," said Lois. "How are you feeling? Sorry you didn't win the money."

"That's okay," laughed Jessie. "It's not why I came here."

"Sure, sure," nodded Lois. "So, what are you going to do when you go home?" Lois mouthed the name "Tom" and nodded encouragingly. She pointed at the camera, prompting Jessie.

Jessie laughed. "I'm going to get in my new Land Rover and drive and drive and drive." She glanced over and caught Nick watching her again but she looked away from him before he could spoil it.

Lois rolled her eyes, and tugged on Kenny's sleeve, pulling him along behind her as she made her way over to Malcolm.

"Any last words?" she asked him.

Malcolm shrugged his shoulders. "I really enjoyed this chance to prove myself. It's back to ordinary life now."

"Very profound," muttered Lois, going after Cindi who was surrounded by fawning cameramen.

Jessie watched out of the corner of her eye as Malcolm went over to Nick. He held out his hand.

"I wanted to say thanks for everything. Thanks for this opportunity."

Nick smiled broadly as he shook Malcolm's hand. "Look," he said, "I know you've got this idea that somehow having kids and living your life isn't very adventurous, but...well, the thing is that my dad was always my greatest hero. He was always there for me, always encouraging me and I knew he always had my back."

Jessie watched Malcolm's face light up.

"There are more ways to prove yourself than wrestling wild animals," said Nick, smiling.

Malcolm laughed, clapping Nick on the shoulder.

Jessie shook her head as she watched Nick walk down to the shore. He was proving relentless at frustrating her efforts to dislike him. She took off her microphone, squared her shoulders and walked down after him. Not to try and talk to him—she knew there was no point in that—but there was one more thing she had to tell him.

He glanced at her as she approached and then looked back towards the ocean, folding his arms.

"Hi," she said. "Look, I just wanted to say thank-you for this whole trip. I know things got a bit complicated—"

He snorted and she winced. "I don't really know what to say about all that, but I did want to say thanks for the other stuff. It probably won't mean anything to you, but this trip really did change my life, and I owe a lot of that to you. The challenges and the survival stuff, I mean, I really enjoyed that."

"I'm sorry you didn't win the money," he said gruffly.

Jessie's shoulders sagged. He really didn't know her at all. She turned away.

"Despite all your varied efforts."

Jessie stopped, brought up short by the sarcastic tone. She knew that the noble thing would just be to ignore his taunt and walk away. Just leave him and his insinuations behind and get on with her life.

She hesitated, catching her lip between her teeth. Nope, she couldn't do it. She turned to face him.

"Well, maybe if I'd slept with you *on* camera," she snapped, "I would have won."

Nick looked taken aback. "What?"

"Yeah," she said, warming up. "Maybe if I'd given Lois and the audience something to look at, I'd have scooped the money. But I guess it took a better woman than me. Or maybe she was just more desperate."

"What are you talking about?"

"Oh, don't play dumb." Jessie gave him a sarcastic smile. "Kenny showed me the tape."

"What tape?"

"*The* tape," said Jessie, as if explaining to a child. "The tape of you and Cindi. After the hot tub. 'Come on, let's get you to bed.'" Jessie waved her hand. "Fortunately, Kenny didn't expect me to watch anymore. But I'm sure it'll be available on video by the time I get home."

"Me and Cindi?" said Nick, his face a mask of bewilderment.

"What?" said Jessie. "You're surprised that I know about it? How could you think that I wouldn't? You've practically been rubbing my face in it."

"There's nothing going on between me and Cindi."

Jessie laughed at his gall. "Oh, you only slept with her, is that it? Of course, that doesn't mean anything to you. I should know that."

"I didn't sleep with Cindi," Nick insisted again.

Jessie opened her mouth for another vehement retort but then she paused, scrutinizing his face.

"What?" she said warily.

"I didn't sleep with Cindi."

"Yes, you did."

Nick leaned towards her, giving her a very direct look. "No. I didn't."

Jessie spoke hesitantly. "You didn't? Not that night...after the hot tub?"

Nick's eyes widened. "The same day that we...are you crazy? Of course not." He peered at her, searching her eyes. "Do you really think that I'd do that?"

Jessie looked away, heat rising in her face. "But I thought...Kenny showed me a tape of you taking her to bed."

Nick thought for a moment. "And that's all I did. She was very drunk so I helped her get into her shelter."

"But you were so distant and cold with me the next day," argued Jessie. "I thought..."

Nick looked uncomfortable. "That was because of what you said to Cindi. I heard you and I just thought it was a complete overreaction. I didn't know what had gotten into you."

Jessie frowned, thinking back to the hot tub conversation. She shook her head in confusion. "What did I say?"

"When you grabbed her and yelled at her, outside the *ladies' room.* I saw you, threatening her."

Jessie winced. "Oh. Okay, you're right, that was bad. I felt awful doing it but I thought I had to stop her somehow."

"Stop her?" Nick's brow was furrowed.

"From going after Malcolm."

"What's Malcolm got to do with it?"

Jessie exhaled with exasperation at his opacity. "She was going to seduce Malcolm, remember? That's why I told her to keep away from him."

Nick blinked slowly and then he let out a hollow laugh. "Oh, boy."

"What?"

He looked at her, running a hand over his stubble. "She told me that the fight was about me—that you were telling her to keep away from me."

Jessie's mouth fell open. She fired a look up towards the campsite. "That b—"

"Okay," said Nick, cutting her off. "So that was a misunderstanding, but how can you explain the fact that you had a fiancé? Are you going to tell me that I misinterpreted that somehow?"

She looked back at him. It made her heart hurt to see the faint hope in his eyes—as if he'd almost be willing to accept any preposterous explanation from her if only it meant she hadn't had a fiancé.

She dropped her eyes. "I'm so sorry." She looked up again quickly, giving him the plain truth. "We'd only been seeing each other for about three months and when he saw me off at the airport he asked me to marry him." She shrugged at the absurdity of it. "I was speechless. We'd never even mentioned it before and I had no idea he was taking it that seriously." She pointed at her chest. "I wasn't! So I didn't say anything. I just kind of shook my head and said I had to catch the plane and I left. It was so ridiculous, I couldn't believe he'd said it."

"But then when he showed up on the island..."

"I thought you'd slept with Cindi," explained Jessie with embarrassment. "And I decided that it would serve you right to think that there was someone else in my life as well. It was stupid. I'm so sorry."

Nick exhaled heavily. "So, this whole time, you thought—"

"—and you thought..." she interrupted him.

Nick looked at her and Jessie saw a light come back into his eyes. For the first time she realized how tense his expression had been for the past few days and it thrilled her to see the laugh lines reappear on his face.

"I don't believe this," he said. "I've been going nuts. I was actually sorry that Tom didn't break his legs when he came sliding down the rope. Seeing the two of you together was horrible enough but then it was even worse thinking that I'd been completely wrong about you. After that day at the lagoon—"

"I was stupid," said Jessie, stepping closer to him. "I should have known you wouldn't do that."

Nick put his hand up to cup her face, running his thumb softly along her lower lip. "I'm sorry I thought the worst of you, too."

She smiled. "I forgive you." She could feel her heart thudding in her chest as Nick's other hand encircled her waist and pressed against the small of her back. "What about the cameras?"

"I don't care about the cameras," said Nick, tilting his head towards hers. "From now on, whenever I want to kiss you, I'm going to."

Epilogue

NICK BLINKED AS THE WIND gusted, blowing a swirl of snow-flakes around his face.

"What?" he said, leaning forward.

Kenny raised his voice. "I said, when is the chopper coming back?"

Nick checked his watch. "About another hour."

"I'm starving," complained Kenny.

Nick fumbled in the voluminous pocket of his coat and pulled out a chocolate bar. "Here."

Kenny chewed as he filmed, only the barest circle of skin visible from the depths of his fur-lined hood.

"It's very important to leave air holes in the roof of your igloo," Nick continued, facing the camera. "It'll get very warm inside from the heat of your body and the surface of the walls will melt and freeze over—to form an airtight ice surface. Without air holes you can get a deadly buildup of carbon monoxide."

He stepped back from the icy dome, pointing to the entrance hole. "The last step is building your entrance tunnel, which stops snow from blowing in." He glanced down and smiled as a head emerged in the doorway. "My wife will be happy to do that."

"Your wife is six months pregnant, tough guy," said Jessie, using his arm to pull herself upright. "You can finish it yourself."

They grinned at each other and Nick leaned in to kiss her. Her hair lifted in the wind and he laughed gently, smoothing it down as he pulled her towards him. She put her arms around his neck and their kiss deepened.

Kenny panned the camera away discreetly, focusing on the blue-green glaciers in the distance as he studiously ignored Lois, who was squawking in his headphones to "Get the shot!"

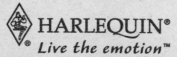

If you enjoyed what you just read,
then we've got an offer you can't resist!

Take 2 bestselling love stories FREE!

Plus get a FREE surprise gift!

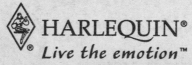